THE $3 MILLION TURN-OVER

The Pro Book One

RICHARD CURTIS

WOLFPACK
PUBLISHING

WOLFPACK PUBLISHING

The $3 Million Turn-Over

Paperback Edition
Copyright © 2020 (As Revised) Richard Curtis

Wolfpack Publishing
6032 Wheat Penny Avenue
Las Vegas, NV 89122

wolfpackpublishing.com

All rights reserved. No part of this book may be reproduced by any means without the prior written consent of the publisher, other than brief quotes for reviews.

This book is a work of fiction. Any references to historical events, real people or real places are used fictitiously. Other names, characters, places and events are products of the author's imagination, and any resemblance to actual events, places or persons, living or dead, is entirely coincidental.

Paperback ISBN 978-1-64734-144-2
eBook ISBN 978-1-64734-057-5
Library of Congress Control Number: 2020944804

THE $3 MILLION TURN-OVER

This is for Marty and Susan

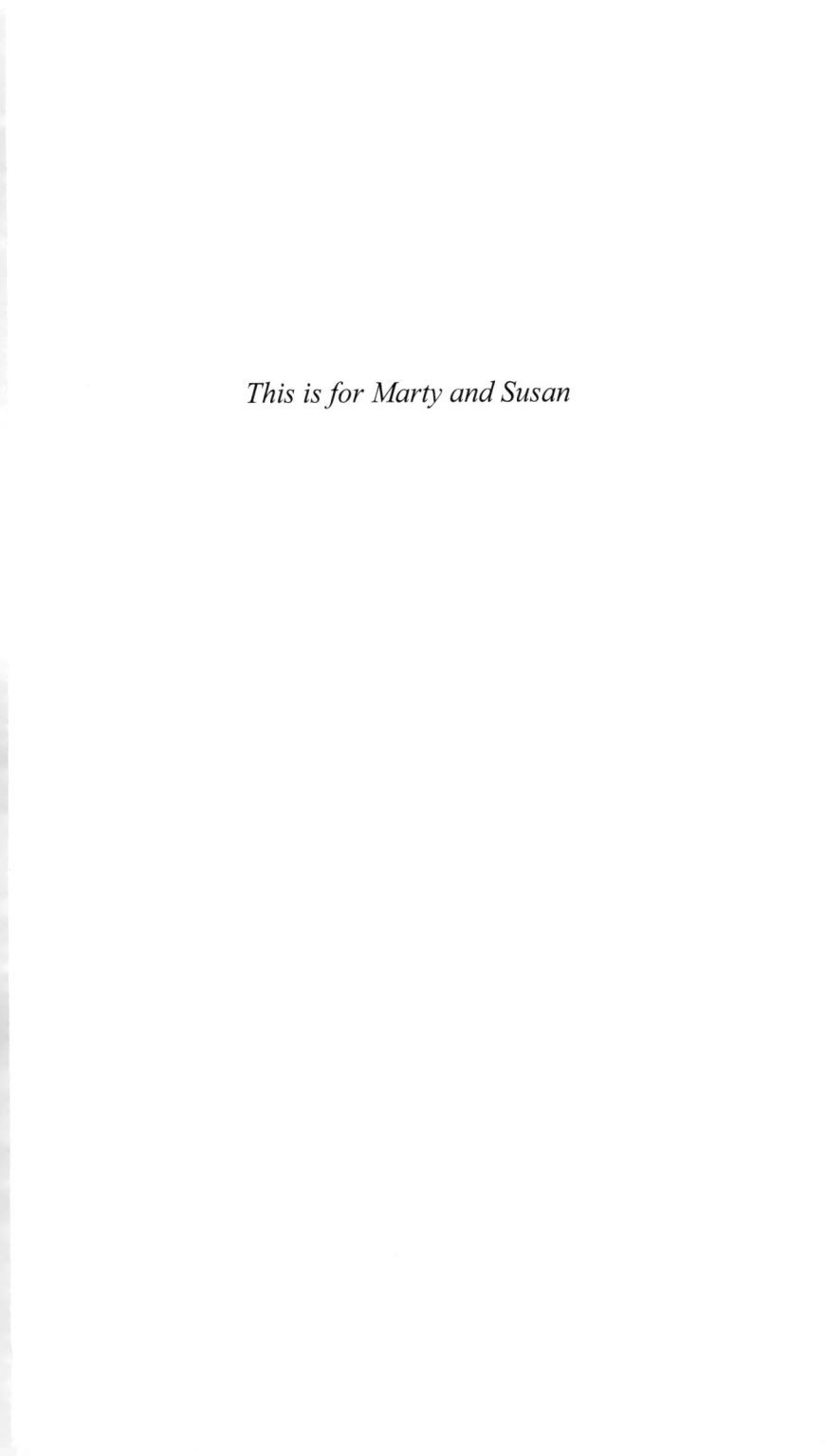

CHAPTER I
....

Call me Ishmael if you want but I answer to the name Dave Bolt. Officially, I'm an agent. I represent professional athletes—baseball players, football players, hockey players, tennis pros, golfers. You name it, if money is paid for any athletic performance short of copulation, I take a commission on it. I represent athletes during negotiations, handle their contracts, line up personal appearances, speeches, and commercial endorsements, advance them money, advance them more money and, when that's gone, advance them still more money. My outfit is called the Red Dog Players Management Agency, which was cute when I had three clients but has become a liability now that I have many more. But you've got to admit it's a name that sticks in your mind.

I say "officially" I'm an agent because in the last couple of years I seem to have backed into another job, an unofficial moonlighting gig and one I'd be just as happy not to have, but it's one of those things where I seem to be the only person qualified to do it. I'm a troubleshooter for a number of pro sports organizations, a kind of undercover operator if you will. Nothing as glorious and glamorous as a private eye, on the contrary, I haven't undertaken a job yet that was anything but a fat pain in the ass. But there are some satisfactions—and some rewards. I help keep the lid on some of the sordid scandals that threaten to wriggle into the public eye and trail slime over what is essentially a decent and noble and beautiful human enterprise. Fixes, drug problems, gangsterism, sex scandals—I try to keep them in the family before the media boys descend and expose some of the uglier seams of professional sports for the world to see. In exchange, the various sports commissions compensate me: a cash bonus here, a referral of a new client there, or some other kind of favor. Sometimes all I get is "Thank You," and sometimes "Thank You" is enough.

"Thank you," for instance, is all I got for finding Richie Sadler and that didn't quite make up for the hairline fracture of my cheekbone, temporary blindness, a scrotum full of somebody's knee, and the loss of the most promising marital prospect I've run across since my divorce. Oh, I did get the right to keep what already belonged to me: a commission of staggering proportions, and as this was my first "case", I also got the reputation for competence among men very high in the sports establishment. But I think that when you hang the whole mess out to dry and take a good look at it, you come up with a great big Who Needed It?

It started early in May with Trish rattling this note under my nose while I was talking to George Allen. Needless to say, I could have brained her. It's hard enough to negotiate with George Allen without having your secretary wave a piece of paper in your face. I made a brushing-away gesture, which any imbecile would have known meant "Get lost!" but she only sighed loudly, put her hands on her hips in profound annoyance and stuck the note under my nose again.

"George, can you hold on one second?" I said into the phone. "I have an inexperienced secretary who thinks there is something more important than talking to you." I punched the "hold" button and glared.

"Inexperienced!" Trish snorted. "I like that!"

"Didn't I say no phone calls?"

"You didn't say *absolutely* no phone calls. I thought you'd want to know about this one."

I looked at the scrawl on the memo pad: "Davis Sadler on 41."

If looks could fire, Trish would have been transported that very second to some shabby employment agency waiting room. "This better be good," I said. "Who's Davis Sadler?"

She looked at me triumphantly. "Richie Sadler's father."

I blinked. It was, as Trish had guessed, perhaps the only call that would justify interrupting a conversation with George Allen. I gazed at the lighted "41" button on my phone panel. Trish did too and said, "That, Mr. Bolt, is a beacon illuminating your destiny."

I tended to agree with her but a principle is a principle and you've got to keep secretaries in their place. If they think they can bust in on important phone calls, the next thing you know they'll be taking five minutes extra on their lunch hours. "Tell Sadler to call back."

Her blue eyes reflected horror. "Are you crazy?"

I rose from my chair. "Do you want to eat your danish with a full set of teeth?" Shaking her head and muttering, she retreated to her desk with long, saucy strides. As I reached for the "40" button on which Allen was holding, I heard her say breathlessly, "Would you mind holding just *one* more second, Mr. Sadler? Mr. Bolt is just wrapping up a *critical* negotiation with George Allen, *the* George Allen of the Washington Redskins . . . Oh you are? Me too. How do you think we look for next fall?" I muttered a silent benediction over Trish's blonde head, she was worth every penny I sometimes paid her.

"Well?" Allen asked. "Was it?"

"Pardon me?"

"Was it more important than talking to me?"

"It could be pretty important," I admitted. "Richie Sadler's father is on the other line."

"Then why don't you take the call?"

"But George..."

"We can wrap this thing up this afternoon. To tell you the truth, I'm curious myself. If it's what I think, it could be quite a feather in your cap."

"*A* feather? George, I could line my nest with feathers if it's what I think."

I hung up and looked at the yellow 41 button for a minute, trying to get my head together. I told myself: *Keep cool, Sadler may not be calling to ask you to represent Richie. Why should he?* But then I asked myself if there were any other reasons that Sadler might want to talk to me. I couldn't think of one.

You didn't have to be a basketball nut to know that Richie Sadler was the hottest professional prospect since UCLA's Bill Walton. In his three varsity years at Illinois, he'd racked up an almost unbelievable 3,200-plus points, averaging 33 points per game, making 66 percent of his field goal attempts, tallying seven 60-point games, and snaring forty zillion rebounds. He'd established an Illinois "dynasty" for the three years he was there, leading the team to a string of victories marred only by a fluke loss to Ohio State in his junior year—fluky because an overly ambitious guard knocked him unconscious with an elbow to the temple early in the third period.

Needless to say, he'd spearheaded the team to three straight NCAA titles and was the All-East American since Dr. Naismith hoisted two peach baskets ten feet above the ground in 1891. By his junior year, sportswriters had run out of superlatives and by the time he was a senior they had ceased comparing him to such classical greats as Mikan and Cousy and Dolph Schayes or white superstars of more recent vintage like Rick Barry and Jerry West and Walton. He was that much in a class by himself. The best the pundits could do was describe him as a "tall" Bill Walton or a "good" Rick Barry. Mostly they called him "Wings" because he seemed to spend more time in the air than on the court and he had that unearthly ability to hang suspended in the midst of a jump shot for longer than the law of gravity says you're supposed to have.

I'd seen Sadler play on a number of occasions at Madison Square Garden and had to confess that in all the time I'd followed the game, I never saw anyone control the ball and dominate the court quite the way he did. For sheer size and bulk he was almost a freak—7'4" and 285 pounds. But he was anything but a clumsy giant. He had a quickness and grace and dazzling speed that made you wonder if he wasn't a fugitive from some extraterrestrial league, the Martian Maulers or the Jupiter Jets or something.

And now Richie Sadler was graduating and was the subject of every conceivable scheme, legal, illegal, and uncategorizable, that could be contrived by teams to both the NBA and ABA to snare him. The salary figures tossed around made your head swim and rattled the composure of even the most cold-blooded players' agents. I was probably the only one of the lot who didn't lose his head, for the simple reason that I didn't have an ice cube's chance in a pizza oven of getting a crack at representing Sadler. Not that I wasn't as good as guys like Al Ross and Bob Woolf and Mark McCormack but my agency was young, small, under financed, understaffed, and underheard of. At that time I didn't have enough clients, especially of the big-name variety, to match my competitors' clout with management or attract other biggies like Sadler. What I did have, at least according to those of my clients who swore by me (when they weren't swearing *at* me), were the following: an intimate inside knowledge of sports, an irrepressible love of athletes, a good head for business, a certain amount of charm and poise and savoir-faire—which really boils down to a rich repertory of filthy jokes—and a reputation among management for fairness. In fact, some of my boys felt I was a management man, that I leaned over backwards to please the owners. I will admit to a strong desire to be on good terms with the people who have the money, I'll even admit to having some compassion for them. Having worked in the front office of the Dallas Cowboys for a couple of years, I am convinced that owners are only 85 percent as monstrous as most players say they are. So while I never give an owner an even break, I occasionally stop short of their jugulars.

Now, these may be admirable qualities per se, but they are not the kind that attract Richie Sadlers. I'm a southern gentleman by upbringing and it's simply not in my nature to go lusting after prospects like a whore in wintertime, phoning them, propositioning them, bothering them at all hours, promising them anything, hustling them, begging them, and even threatening them, like some other members of my fraternity I could name. Dignity, for better or for worse, is my long suit. Unfortunately, dignity isn't worth rat shit when there's a Richie Sadler at stake. So when the sharks started swimming around him, I just stood back and watched with detached amusement and made snide comments about human greed and venality. Trish called them sour grapes.

And now Richie Sadler's father was calling me. *Me!*

I pressed the button and listened for a minute to Trish's astute analysis of the relative merits of Sonny Jurgensen and Billy Kilmer, while Davis Sadler made chauvinistic grunts about how knowledgeable she was for a girl. Knowing how Trish gets on *that* topic, I spoke into the phone. "Um, that'll be fine, Trish. I've got it."

"That you, Bolt?" Sadler's voice was gruff but genial. "Hey, leave that gal on the line. She knows more about sports than Howard Cosell."

Trish threw me a glance over her shoulder and observing the menacing gesture I was making, begged off and hung up. I threw her a kiss. She could not have buttered him up better if she'd been a Scovill Joe Namath corn popper.

"To what do I owe the pleasure, Mr. Sadler?" I said.

"I'm bringing the family to New York for a couple of days and thought we'd meet a few people we haven't met."

"You haven't met enough agents?"

"Met too goddam many of them and that's the problem. I don't trust any of them. They don't give two shits about my son. They just want to get fat off him. I heard you're, well, more of a low-key person. I also heard you were very good."

I thought a little candor wouldn't hurt. "I've got to tell you, Mr. Sadler, I wouldn't mind getting fat on your son's commissions."

"Ah hell, Bolt, I don't begrudge a man his commissions, but I do begrudge him a piece of a kid's soul, do you see my distinction? These other clowns—you wouldn't believe what they've offered us."

"You sound like a sensible man, Mr. Sadler. Who told you about me?"

"Lonnie Seaforth, for one. Lonnie was Richie's idol when Richie was a kid. Now Richie may be playing in the same league with him. You've done a great job for Lonnie and he hasn't become a phony like some other players who've hit it big. Lonnie told Richie you smack him down whenever he starts putting on airs. That impressed us."

I made a mental note to do something extravagant for Lonnie and said, "Well, Mr. Sadler, the temptations at the pro level are mighty powerful. Someone has to maintain his sense of proportion." Trish looked up from her files and performed a digging pantomime number, leaving no doubt in my mind as to what was on the shovel. But I really wasn't mouthing pieties; I've seen too many good kids ruined by instant stardom.

"We're taking a late afternoon flight out of Chicago," Sadler said. "Are you free for dinner tonight?"

"Dinner?" I rattled the pages of my blank appointment calendar. "I've got a tentative engagement but I can move it up to another evening."

"Fine, if that doesn't inconvenience you. Say, do you mind if I bring my wife and daughter along? They want to do their spring shopping in the Big Apple."

"You mean bring them along to dinner? Sure!" I said wincing. Two reminder letters from the Diner's Club bearing huge red-ink warnings of dire action stared me in the face even as I spoke.

"And say, you must bring that gal of yours along too. She's a charmer."

"Trish? I'm not sure she's free." You can imagine Trish's reaction to *that*. Then I thought about it and decided she might be just the extra special ingredient to consummate the deal. "No, she says she can make it," I said picturing the night's tab soaring deep into the three-digit stratosphere.

"Would you prefer someplace quiet or noisy?"

"It doesn't matter," Sadler said with an air of resignation. "We're going to be recognized wherever we go. You can't exactly hide Richie. Just pick a good place. We'll phone you when we get in."

I hung up and looked at Trish. "How'd you like to be my date tonight?"

"Only if it includes sleeping with you."

She was hunkered down putting some papers in a low file drawer. Her skirt rode up high on her thighs, exposing the moons of her tight little buttocks rimmed with blue panties. I stared and she knew I stared and I felt the same tingle of desire I'd had for her on the average of five times a week for the last year. She had smashingly long legs and loved to show them off with mini-skirts—even though "sensible" lengths had been the proper mode for the past five years. She had small high breasts and loved to show *them* off with bra-less sweaters, semi-sheer blouses, and clingy jersey halters. She had this steady boyfriend, Marvin or Melvin or some name like that, with whom she slept regularly but that didn't seem to make much difference to her. Had I given her so much as an eye-flick of encouragement, she'd have gone to bed with me or even to floor or to desk.

And eventually I'd have had to fire her, which is why I hadn't given her so much as an eye-flick of encouragement.

"Sorry, sweetheart," I said, averting my eyes at last. "I told you what my daddy used to say."

She sighed. "I know: 'Son, never shit where you eat.' "

"That's right. Not that it wouldn't be a pleasure..."

"...and a privilege to spend the night with me, right? Oh, these courtly southerners," she groaned... "Where shall I make the reservation?"

"How about Maxwell's Plum?"

"Well, if they don't care about being seen, that's perfect."

Maxwell's Plum is one of my favorite restaurants in New York City. It sprang up on First Avenue and 64th Street in the midst of the explosive migration of young people to the Upper East Side and became one of the most popular spots along that fabulous row of singles bars, discos, and restaurants familiarly known as "The Strip." Then the chic people discovered it and the management revamped its cuisine and service (and prices, of course) to cater to the carriage trade. But it still retains its attraction for hungry young bachelors and single girls; the mixture of fat cats dining on the upper level and colorful commoners conducting their courtship rites around the bar below is what makes Maxwell's as close to a fashionable Paris *boite as* New York can claim.

Trish and I arrived five minutes before our 7:30 reservation and waited on the stairs to the upper level for the maitre d' to usher us to our table. Trish primped before the mirrored wall and I couldn't help thinking what a nice couple we made. She was 23, but a mature 23, and I was 35 but could pass for 34 in a dimly lit room. She was fairly tall, about 5 feet 7, so she didn't make my 6-feet, 3-inches stature look excessively awkward. She was pretty—that night she was positively scintillating in a scoop-necked jobbie that fell away from her white breasts whenever she (or I) turned this way or that—and I, to be perfectly immodest, wasn't half bad if you like rugged looks and are not too particular about noses that appear to have been broken six times but set only five. Trish was blonde and I was blond, except her hair was long and straight and mine tightly curled—almost kinky, if you will.

It's a funny thing about my almost kinky hair. Portraits of my forebears—and the Bolts go back a long, long way—show the traditional straight blond hair and fair complexion of the classical Anglo-Saxon. Then my great-great-grandfather pops up with kinky hair and a swarthy complexion. Interesting, wot? Could it have anything to do with the fact that my great-great-grandfather's daddy owned a dozen slaves?

It's my speculation, therefore, that one-drop of blood out of every 32 that courses through my veins is not Caucasian. Which may account for a lot of otherwise inexplicable things about me such as how I'm able to be on scandalously chummy terms with black people.

The maitre d' led us to a big table by the railing separating the balconied dining area from the bar and while we waited for our guests, we indulged in daydreams about what it would be like to land Richie Sadler as a client. Some of these were pretty fantastic, yet when we thought about them some more, they seemed perfectly capable of realization. For Richie Sadler was potentially a pivotal—no pun intended—figure in modern basketball history. Some said he held the key to its future and that key was worth millions.

From the birth in 1967 of the American Basketball Association in rivalry with the "establishment" National Basketball Association, the two leagues had been conducting a costly and sometimes vicious salary war. Ethics, such as they were, went completely down the crapper as owners flaunted eligibility rules, conducted illegal drafts, and stole, seduced, bought, and all but shanghaied each other's stars. Veteran players jumped leagues and hot collegiate prospects finessed astronomical bonuses and salaries. High school and even pre-high school kids were wined and dined five or even ten years ahead of eligibility and whenever they shook hands with a pro scout they always seemed to come away with money stuck mysteriously to their palms.

Merger had been proposed as a solution, the owners generally favoring it because it would deflate salaries and kill the price war, the players opposing it for the same reason. The question of merger also foundered on the shoals of prestige; the NBA didn't feel the ABA was good enough. And big television money backed up NBA's snobbery. The NBA had a network contract, the ABA did not, and that really hurt.

Everybody agreed, therefore, that it would probably take a superstar, the basketball equivalent of a Joe Namath, to make a merger feasible. It had almost happened in 1969 when Lew Alcindor was drafted by the teams with the poorest records in both the NBA and ABA, the Milwaukee Bucks and the New York Nets respectively. Alcindor restricted the bidding to one offer each and actually hoped the Nets would get him because he loved New York. But the Bucks came through with the higher bid, $1.4 million, and merger talk immediately faded. But a few years later, it began building to a crescendo again, with superstars like Julius Erving ramrodding ABA teams that were every bit as good as anything the NBA could field. By the time Richie Sadler came along, merger fever was once more in the air.

I forgave myself for letting my imagination carry me away.

At about 7:40 a collective gasp from the "plummies" crowded around the bar heralded the arrival of my would-be meal ticket. His murmured name rippled through the restaurant as the giant was quickly identified. I must say I was as awed as anybody in the room. It's one thing to see a basketball player on the court with other basketball players, it's quite another to see him lumber into an environment populated by mere mortals. I've been out to dinner with some pretty lofty men. Among my clients are four basketball players 6-foot-6 or bigger and several football behemoths easily mistakable for Reo tractor-trailers. But Richie had a dimension all his own and as he approached our table, trailed by his parents and sister, I knew what the *Titanic's* captain must have felt when a certain iceberg loomed over his beam.

Richie's retinue was no collection of midgets by any means. Richie's father, himself a former collegiate basketball player of some note, was well above 6-feet tall, though a substantial paunch detracted from the overall impression. The mother, a floridly dressed, brassy-looking broad with Midwest Nouveau Riche stamped across her hard face, was close to 6-feet tall herself. Sis was the shortest of the lot at about 5-9. She was also the biggest surprise. For some reason, I'd expected the traditional pigtailed kid sister but she was older than Richie by, I'd say, three or four years. More significantly, she was a very attractive young lady. She wore a modest but tasteful linen pantsuit with a ruffled blouse but it couldn't conceal a willowy figure that seemed to drift over the carpet as if shock absorbers were implanted in her joints. Her face was oval with high cheekbones. Her hair was dark, her eyes green and observant. Unfortunately, the mouth spoiled it, not because it wasn't pretty but because it was puckered in a resentful pout. She looked like a girl with a chip on her shoulder.

All eyes focused on me as I stood to welcome the Sadlers. We shook hands and made our introductions and, with some difficulty, settled into our seats. Seating Richie Sadler, to use another maritime simile, is like berthing an ocean liner. Either his knees lift the table clear off the floor or his outstretched feet create major disruptions within a five-foot radius. But after a minute or two of musical ankles, we finally got settled. Predictably, some jerk, a leering, flower-shirted dude in his forties who should have known better, sidled up to the railing and asked the inevitable: "How's the weather up there, Wings?"

Trish, God bless her, dipped her fingers into her water and flicked a spray of droplets into the guy's face. "Inclement, you little schmuck," she snapped. The place dissolved in laughter as he skulked back to the bar.

"I told you she was a charmer," Davis Sadler beamed at his family. He studied Trish in a distinctly unfatherly way.

I took drink orders with my usual urbanity while sizing the Sadler clan up out of the corner of my eye.

Davis and Bea Sadler looked like typical well-to-do Midwesterners on the surface, open-faced, friendly, a little loud and vulgar, bewildered and flattered by the prodigious attention bestowed on them ever since Richie's genetic messengers had fucked up an order to stop his growth at 6-1. I guess you could describe the Sadlers as Babbitts. But then the Babbitts, if I recollect my Sinclair Lewis rightly, were no simps and like their literary counterparts these two had shrewd, hawk-like eyes, the eyes of opportunists and between happy-go-lucky twinkles, they examined me with clinical severity. I reminded myself that I was not there to entertain, whatever I reported officially to the Internal Revenue Service, and though I laughed a lot and loudly I kept my guard high against probing jabs that might catch me flatfooted.

Richie was one of those kids you like right off the bat, a tousle-haired titan with soft friendly eyes and a voice and manner that proclaimed sincerity with every word and gesture. He seemed (and in the next couple of hours would prove) to be courteous, modest, well-spoken, and intelligent. He confirmed everything I had read and heard about him and in the previous few hours, I had read and heard a great deal.

Immediately after his father phoned, I'd done some crash research on Richie. I didn't merely want facts and statistics but color, so I could formulate a three-dimensional picture of his personality and know what breed of cat I was dealing with. What emerged sounded approximately like a page out of *Lives of the Saints*. If I had what he had, I'd have become more egocentric than Caligula. He attracted money and power like a bull does heifers in season and where there's that much money and power, you'll always see greed and corruption billowing around it. Yet he had not been tainted. While he was still in high school, some three hundred colleges had offered him every inducement you can name: scholarships, loans, cars, broads, even boats and airplanes. But he had walked away from all of them. At length, he chose to go to Illinois, his father's alma mater. "I like its academic and athletic tradition," *Sport* quoted him as saying, "and I feel a strong loyalty to the state I was born and raised in." The article went on to catalogue Richie's virtues which included but were not limited to humility, maturity, fairness, patriotism, and piety.

The title of the *Sport* piece was, "Is This Kid for Real?"

That was the question I'd asked Lonnie Seaforth when I phoned him in Cleveland to thank him for the recommendation and asked him what he thought of Richie. "Oh yes, he's for real, Dave. As upright as an oak and slightly taller."

"Come on, Lonnie. Surely somewhere along the way he accepted a dime for a phone call?"

"Uh-uh."

"A car? A motorcycle? A trike?"

"Nope."

"A little stinky-pinky with some homecoming queen?"

"Dave, you don't understand, the kid *has* all that. His father's regional director of an insurance company and pulls down close to six figures. Richie wants a car, Richie *gets* a car. Richie wants a motorboat, Richie *gets* a motorboat. Scholarships? What does he need them for? He's got the brains to make any college he wants on his own hook—and his old man has the tuition. He sends scholarship offers back saying they should go to the kids who really need them. And girls? Baby, he just has to wrinkle his nose and he has twenty pussies *presenting* to him! Look, man, Richie isn't some poor, ignorant ghetto cat who goes berserk when he lays his hands on some big-league bread. We're talking about an upper-middle-class WASP with every privilege a kid could want."

I shook my head in disbelief. "Surely he must have a flaw or a problem or a vice or something, Lonnie. I mean, even the Messiah had a few hang-ups."

My client paused and thought about it. "Well, Richie does have one serious problem."

"Aha! What's that?"

"He only hits 82 percent of his free throws."

"I knew he was too good to be true," I grinned. Then I fingered a *New York Daily News* clipping that had provoked my curiosity. "What about this Kentucky thing?"

"You mean The Non-Game of the Decade? Oh, God," Lonnie moaned, "You're not going to bring *that* up."

"It sounded pretty fantastic to me," I admitted.

"Fantastic? The *News* is lucky Richie didn't sue them off the face of the planet."

I looked at the clipping again. It was an item by a writer named Harry Leggett whose articles were no more inaccurate than those of most other sportswriters, which is to say it was a mélange of rumors, guesses, hunches, hopes, dreams, inventions, and occasionally, a correctly spelled name.

It was about last winter's NCAA tournament final and as bizarre a mismatch as you're ever likely to see. Richie's Illini deserved to be there, of course, but the Kentucky Wildcats had reached the final rung on the wings of incredible luck. One of their opponents simply came out shooting cold, another was smitten with the flu, the next lost its star forward when he cracked a wrist bone slipping in his bathtub, etc. But alas, the Cinderella story seemed to be about to come to a shattering halt the night of the final. The Illini was healthy, up for the game, and, if their warmup was any indication, a lead-pipe cinch to make off with the title by at least twenty points. The official point spread, determined by The Greek in Vegas, was fifteen. And guess what? Illinois creamed Kentucky, 88-51. Forty-eight of the winning points were scored by Richie Sadler.

No surprise, right? Well, it seems that a gambler named Manny Ricci had put up a ton of money, much of it belonging to an underworld syndicate, on Kentucky, taking the 15-point spread. And he had lost every last red cent. Thereupon, he howled that he'd "gotten" to Richie Sadler and Richie was, for a consideration, supposed to shave points and keep the spread below 15. Richie had, in other words, double-crossed him.

"Don't you see?" Lonnie said. "Ricci lost his huge bundle and needed a reason, any reason, why the mob shouldn't cut his heart out with a dull instrument, such as the heel of a shoe with a foot still in it. So Ricci invented this . . . this breathtakingly terrible story about Richie Sadler. I guarantee you, the only reason Ricci is still alive is he's probably sworn to make the money good to his boss. As soon as he does, you'll read about a 'gangland fashion slaying' with Ricci turning up one part at a time on the Hackensack Meadows. Let me tell you something, Dave, we become so cynical, we don't recognize the genuine article when it turns up."

"Genuine article?"

"A good person, a decent human being. Richie Sadler is such a one. Treat him like one."

"I haven't got him yet."

"I think you will. You're a genuine article yourself."

"That's kind of you, Lonnie. What do you want?"

"Brut is looking for a basketball star to do a commercial. Can you get me a whaddyacallit, an audition?"

"Sure," I laughed.

"*I* never claimed to be the genuine article," Lonnie said.

The only Sadler who gave me a fuzzy reading was the sister, Sondra. What was behind that frown on her lips and why did those heartbreaking green eyes appraise me so suspiciously? I had to find out before I blundered into some fatal error of diplomacy.

"And what do *you* think of all this brouhaha over your brother?" I asked her.

"You really want to know?"

"I don't ask questions capriciously," I said.

"I haven't heard you ask any other way," she replied.

I must have been an interesting sight, sitting there with this silly-ass grin frozen on my face.

Trish came to my rescue. Poking a cautionary toe into my shinbone, she said, "Oh, Mr. Bolt is simply in his 'charming host' bag tonight, Sondra. Deep down, he's a man who doesn't ask questions capriciously." That cracked the girl's frown slightly and Trish followed up with, "You think this whole thing's a drag, don't you?"

"You don't know what we've been through with these agents, all day, all night—*byechh*." She actually shuddered. She looked at me with open hostility and, of course, now I had her pegged. She obviously pictured herself as the one sane head in the family, the bearer of the Torah of common sense in a world that had lost its head over her brother. This was Richie's protectress, his shield against corruption. And in her eyes, I was just as big a carrier of the contagion as every other agent she'd met.

Trish looked at Sondra sincerely and said, "You don't have any reason to believe this but I want you to know Dave Bolt is not One of the *byechhy* agents."

I looked at Trish and said, "That's one of the nicest things anybody's ever said about me. I'm going to have it chiseled on my tombstone."

I caught Sondra smiling out of the corner of my eye and breathed easier. The first squall had passed, my boat had been rocked but it hadn't shipped much water.

I ordered dinner and did my best not to flinch when the Sadlers asked for lobsters. Now, lobsters are so expensive these days that most restaurants are afraid to list the prices. I'd been reading the menu from right to left starting with the prices but then decided what the hell, if I got Richie Sadler for a client, I'd buy the whole lobster industry and as much of the Atlantic Ocean as was necessary to sustain it. "Lobsters all around," I said with an artless flourish to the headwaiter. "And a couple of bottles of Piper-Heidseck, preferably 1967."

Over appetizers, we passed the time of day with gossip. Few basketball personalities, agents, owners, salaries, and scandals were left unturned. I don't believe I scored too badly in this preliminary. Dinner was served and I kept conversation light, being of the school that says business is best conducted on a full stomach. Trish was wonderful, gabbing about the comparative merits of Bloomingdale's and Bonwit's and Bendel's and finally offering to take the two women shopping the following day. I was pretty wonderful myself, telling some naughty anecdotes about my days as a Dallas Cowboy and even managing to elicit some honest-to-goodness laughter from Sondra.

All this time I was inching up on The Big Question and taking further readings of wind direction and velocity. By dessert time, it was clear it was blowing strongly out of Davis Sadler's seat. It seemed that every time I asked Richie a question of any importance, his father answered for him. Richie appeared to accept this situation complacently enough and so more and more I found myself addressing his father. Sadler had slowly dropped the Babbitt routine and revealed himself to be an ambitious, calculating man guided—I might almost say driven—by a single-minded vision of his son as the quintessential basketball hero, the archetype by which all players past, present, and future would be measured, in short, the All-Time Greatest. It was kind of scary, how much he wanted for the boy. It was easy to see why so many other agents had fallen short of the mark, they'd only promised him the moon and that wasn't good enough. My problem was, I couldn't make promises, except promises to try.

Dessert came, then coffee, and then we went onto after-dinner drinks and I wondered if we were ever going to get around to what we were all there for. But at last, Sadler nudged the ash out of the Upmann I'd given him—I keep a small cache of contraband Cuban cigars for just such occasions—and said, "Well, Bolt what do you think?"

"Think?"

"About Richie? About what's the best thing to do?"

It was a straightforward enough question but ringed with more traps than the 17th hole at Pebble Beach. If I blithely proposed the *wrong* best thing to do I could end up with six buttery lobster bibs and no client. "It depends on how Richie feels about it," I said evasively. "Let's review his options. He's been drafted by the Boston Bombers of the ABA and the Newark Nationals of the NBA. They were both terrible last year but, of course, that was their first year as expansion teams. Whichever Richie plays for, he's going to turn it around."

"Like Kareem turned the Milwaukee Bucks around," Trish said. In his rookie year Lew Alcindor, now Kareem Abdul-Jabbar, took a team that had won only 27 games the year before and led them to 56 wins and second place in the Eastern division of the NBA.

Richie looked appreciatively at Trish, then shrugged. "I kind of prefer Boston to Newark. Even though Newark is closer to New York, Boston is much more beautiful and has so many cultural advantages."

"Don't forget," I said, "you don't have to play for either. If you wanted to play for another team, it wouldn't be hard for me to arrange for you to be traded."

I looked at Richie's father. He wore an impatient expression. "It's not the team, it's the league that counts and I'd like to see him go with the ABA if we can get a good price." He puffed on his cigar, wreathed himself in blue smoke, and looked up at Maxwell's stunning stained-glass ceiling "Wouldn't it be something if the leagues merged because of *my* son."

There it was: *The* Fantasy. Now I had my instructions and the path was clear. "They're almost there now. All it will take is—well, a Richie Sadler."

"Oh, this is doing wonders for his humility," Sis groaned.

It was too bad, but for the moment Sis would have to be sacrificed. "Darling," I said, "the day your kid brother dribbled his first basketball he sealed his fate. Unless he's prepared to give up the game completely, there's only one direction he can go, and that's to the pinnacle. If I get to be his agent, I'll do all I can to keep his head from swelling but I'm afraid you're going to have to get used to his attracting more attention than Pickett's charge at Gettysburg."

Sadler studied me respectfully. I had spoken in terms that fulfilled his astronomical aspirations. But his eyes were still clouded with indecision. "Let me ask you a plain question, Bolt. Why should you be Richie's agent instead of any of the fifty other people we've talked to?"

I'd been afraid he'd ask that. I looked into my brandy glass for an answer. I found brandy in it. "You know what, Mr. Sadler? I don't know why, myself. The best I can tell you is, I'm as good as anybody else."

There was an eerie silence, not just at the table but, it seemed, throughout the restaurant as if no one could believe I wouldn't lay on just a little bullshit to land this client. Then Trish slashed the air with her hand. "He's better than anybody else, Mr. Bolt. He can not only swing a deal as big as any of those other guys but he has something most of them don't even know the meaning of."

"What's that?" Sadler asked.

"Compassion."

I gulped. "Come on, Trish, nobody wants to hear about that."

She talked right over me. "Would you like to know why Dave isn't rolling in money? Because he gives most of it away. I can name ten of his clients who would be up the creek without a paddle if Dave hadn't advanced them money, or loaned it, or simply given it to them. He *cares* what happens to his boys, Mr. Sadler. That's something money can't buy."

Trish's peroration echoed in the well of silence that ensued and I held my breath waiting for something to happen. Trish downed her brandy in one shot and looked at me nervously as Richie and mommy and daddy and sis exchanged searching glances and seemed to be determining something by that magical intuitive process that close families have.

At length, Mrs. Sadler made the only non-shopping reference she'd expressed during the entire evening. "I think that's nice, that Mr. Bolt cares."

It was so ludicrous I almost laughed but, apparently, it was an articulation of something much more profound than I had imagined, for the next thing I knew Davis Sadler was saying, "Is your office near here?"

Trying to maintain some semblance of cool, I said, "A short cab ride away."

"Maybe we should continue this discussion up there."

"I'll call for the check," I said, trying not to sound delirious.

CHAPTER II

• • • •

"Is there anything else I can do for you folks?" I asked, handing Trish the executed letter of agreement and directing her to put it in the safe. "Theater tickets? Or perhaps you'd like to take in a Yankee game?

The women, content with the next day's shopping spree, shrugged, and Davis Sadler said no thanks, he had some other business to attend to, but Richie scuffed the carpet with his size 475 shoe and said, "I have a kind of freaky request, Mr. Bolt."

No perversion is too vile for my new client, I said to myself. *He likes little boys, I'll fix him up with my nephew.* "What's that?"

He gave a nervous staccato laugh. "Well, I brought my sneakers with me, and . . ."

I gasped. "You want to play basketball?"

"Up in Harlem."

"Harlem? Ah." For connoisseurs of basketball, the finest games next to those on the professional courts are to be found in ghetto schoolyards. Almost every great black pro got his start in the half-court one-on-ones or three-on-threes played year-round in playgrounds in every kind of weather short of blizzard and many pros play there for fun or practice or run clinics and tournaments during the off-season.

"I've played with a lot of black guys in college but they all say if I want to know what the game's all about, I should try my luck in a Harlem schoolyard." He looked at me apologetically. "There's not much of a ghetto in Evanston..."

"I'll pick you up at 10 tomorrow morning," I said. "Bring your sneakers and some Band-Aids, but leave your 'white' bag at the hotel."

The next morning, Saturday, was a gorgeous May Day, the sycamores that shade the city's sidewalks glowing a bright chartreuse in the full flush of spring.

The St. Regis Hotel was rather scandalized as Richie and I ambled through its gilded lobby dressed in faded jeans, T-shirts and sneakers. We could have taken my car or a taxi but that would have been inappropriate so we walked down 55th Street to Madison Avenue and caught a No. 2 bus uptown. I pointed out some of the more elegant shops along the way but the closer we got to 96th Street, the dividing line between "downtown" and "uptown," the shabbier things looked. We passed Mount Sinai Hospital and plunged into teeming, garbage-strewn East Harlem. The bus turned up 110th Street, skirting the northern boundary of Central Park and redeeming us from squalor for a short while. Then it made a right at Seventh Avenue. "Welcome to Harlem," I said.

We got off the bus near 130th Street and walked toward a large blacktop schoolyard on the corner. Needless to say, Richie was the object of many stares and whispers. I wasn't particularly uptight but I thought Richie might be. "Walk tall, son," I said.

"It would be hard for me to walk any other way, Mr.

Bolt," he said under his breath.

Richie seemed visibly to relax as the drumming of basketballs and the *sproing* of vibrating hoops and the blare of rock music grew louder. We came to a chicken wire fence with torn gaps wide enough to drive a taxi through. At the moment, the yard was occupied by half a dozen scrappy half-court games played by twelve-and thirteen-year-olds but in one corner some very tall and muscular adults were warming up and a knot of spectators was forming around them. Many heads turned as we stepped through the fence and in the ensuing buzz, I heard Richie's name mentioned several times. But our only greeting was a collective stare of curiosity. I searched the yard for some face I knew and after a moment spied the one in particular I'd been hoping to find. My eyes caught his and he gave me a big smile as he pushed through the little crowd.

"That's Tatum Farmer I was telling you about," I said to Richie as we met my friend halfway. Tatum was a tall, well-built dude, almost bald but with a ruff of shiny black hair around his head and a fulsome brushy mustache that hadn't been affected by aging the way his head had been. He was wearing orange shorts and a faded blue-and-orange sweatshirt that said, "Property of Syracuse University." When he grinned he displayed a bright gold cap on one of his front teeth. Tatum was one of my oldest friends, going back to college days when we'd beaten the other's brains out in the 1960 Cotton Bowl, Syracuse winning over the Longhorns, 23-14. He was a terrific all-around athlete but after a couple of years in professional football and a few more with the old American Basketball League, he'd dropped out and gotten involved in community work. Aside from being one of the nicest and most dedicated men you'd ever want to know, he'd introduced me to a lot of prospects who eventually became my clients.

"What's happenin', Lightning?" he said, slapping my palm and referring to me by one of my many nicknames. I've been called "Thunder," "Blue," and the other inevitable nicknames that combine with the last name Bolt. I was also called "Sleeper" when I was in high school and "Bum" when I left the Dallas Cowboys for a two-year plunge into the bottom of a bourbon bottle.

"How you doin', Tatum?"

"Come to play some basketball with the brothers, have you?"

"I thought I might if you got some burnt-out cases I can keep up with."

"Aw, bullshit, Dave, you can hold your own with any teen-age hot dog out here." He looked up at my companion. "Here's a kid looks just like Richie Sadler."

"That's who it is," I said.

"Hello, Wings," Tatum said, extending his hand. "You sure were something else in that North Carolina semifinal. Next day I had six or eight kids down here trying to imitate that left-handed fadeaway you done in the third period."

"I'm not sure I could do it again myself," Richie said. "The fact is, I was off-balance and somebody was clinging to my right wrist... Any chance of my getting into a game?"

"Are you kidding? It would be an honor. Too bad you weren't here last week. We had Hawk and Clyde down here. Good God Almighty, they made the asphalt *smoke!*"

Richie's eyes widened. "Connie Hawkins and Walt Frazier? Oh wow!"

Tatum smiled. "You'd best quit oh-wowing, son, you're gonna be playing against the likes of them next year. Anyway, ain't nobody here today. Just some good amateurs. Should be sittin' ducks for the Great White Hope."

The way Tatum said it, with a warm, teasing smile, no one could mistake it for antagonism. But it did serve to remind Richie he was in for more than his usual quota of thrown elbows, knees and hips as some of the bloods tried to make their reps by taking him down.

"I don't see any sitting ducks," Richie said, surveying the men warming up.

"Oh, they'll make you sweat some," Tatum replied.

"Got anyone interesting you want me to see?" I asked him as we walked onto the court.

"As a matter of fact, there is. We'll be playing with him today. Name of Timmie Lee. That's him."

He nodded at a sullen kid with an extravagant naturally tall, beanpole body. With his huge hands and feet, he looked like an awkward puppy but if he grew into them the way a puppy grows into its oversized paws, this was going to be one heckuva big human being. As it was he stood out strikingly against the several adults practicing under the backboard.

"How much of him is hair?" I asked Tatum.

"Everything but 6-4. Look at him move, Dave. Lookit, lookit." Timmie had just sliced through an imaginary crowd of defenders, faked a left-handed layup and caromed a right-handed shot.

"I like him," I said.

"Damn right you like him and you'll be happy to have 10 percent of him one of these days. But I wish you'd talk to him."

"That's not ethical."

"No, I don't mean that. I mean, well, I'm worried about him."

"Drugs?"

"No, thank God. But he's fallin' in with the wrong type of people."

Before Tatum could explain, his friends got on him to get the game started. We wedged through the crowd of spectators, which was now considerable and Tatum did the introductions. A couple of the guys I'd played with before but most of them I didn't know. Richie was greeted respectfully but not overenthusiastically. He may have been a national figure but up here, as the saying goes, that don't mean shit. A man has to prove himself all over again when he plays in a Harlem schoolyard and every one of these guys could boast of having outscored or out-rebounded or outfought or outhustled men making as much as $100,000 a year playing professional basketball. It was common to hear cocky ghetto ballplayers boast, "Maybe he leads the league but he didn't show me *nuthin'* out here."

Sides were chosen and Richie and I ended up on opposing teams. Timmie Lee, the kid Tatum was so high on, was on my side. He seemed incapable of standing still. He paced and shuffled and jitterbugged nervously waiting for the game to begin, like a boxer anticipating the bell. "Take it easy, my man, you'll wear out your sneakers before we begin," I told him. He looked at me humorlessly and said nothing.

It was a full-court, five-on-five, 21-point game. No referee, of course. Disputes were to be settled by a combination of the honor system and rough justice. Oddly enough, it works most of the time. People who think of the ghetto as a hotbed of lawlessness ought to watch a schoolyard basketball game.

The game started off a little pokily, with the two sides cautiously feeling each other out, finding the range and getting a sense of what the opposition could and could not do. Timmie Lee was assigned to guard Richie and came on like a fighting bantam, covering him with flailing hands and ever-shifting feet. Richie played woodenly for the first few minutes and in fact, seemed dazzled and intimidated by Timmie. He passed off a lot and preferred to shoot from the outside rather than risk a drive. On offense, Timmie very decidedly outhustled my new client, using his needle-sharp elbows to barge past Richie for layups. We jumped out to a 7-3 lead, two of our points the contribution of yours truly on not-half-bad jumpers from the corner over the outstretched hands of Tatum Farmer.

Richie, sweating heavily in the close, climbing late-morning heat, threw off his shirt, revealing a number of nasty red bruises on the fair skin of his chest and arms. He'd taken a lot of licks already and the game was still young. Yet he'd refused to call even flagrant fouls or get overly physical himself, I think because he was loath to win on chickenshit calls or cheap shots. I admired that but when he continued holding, back I began to wonder about him. His teammates began feeding to Bubba Norris, their captain, who was a head shorter than Richie but unafraid of plowing through a gauntlet of angry hands. Norris kept them almost on a par with us and after about 10 minutes we were ahead by only 2 points.

We took a break at 11 points and I listened to the murmurs in the crowd. They were distinctly critical and even contemptuous of Richie and I felt embarrassed for him. I knew he was holding back but putting myself in his place I could easily see how a white giant playing in the most physical game of his life in front of a rabid and racially partisan crowd might feel more than a little at sea. One remark floated out of the perimeter of spectators and I know Richie heard it, for he jerked his head as if stung by a hornet. "Timmie Lee's blowin' the white dude away." It was followed by unsuppressed chortles and handclaps and Richie's face reddened. He looked at me with bewildered eyes.

Timmie Lee heard it too and darted a look of triumph at his supporters. When play resumed he came out doing a kind of Ali shuffle, clearly intending to humiliate his opponent.

That was a mistake.

Richie's lips pursed angrily and his eyes narrowed with indignation. I realized that he'd been dogging it out of fear of taking advantage of amateurs and kids. It had just dawned on him that they had no similar compunctions. He had just discovered the difference between the game they play in Evanston, IL, and the one they play on Seventh Avenue and 130th Street, New York City. In the former, you want to win, in the latter, you have to. He'd learned what he'd come here to learn and now he was ready to play basketball.

He took a deep breath and gave a sharp shake of the head and I could almost hear the hang-ups clattering out onto the blacktop. He said something to his teammates.

They brought the ball down and after working it around for a while, Bubba Norris fed it high to Richie. In just two gigantic strides he roared into the keyhole like the *Santa Fe Chief* and stuffed the ball so hard and true it bounced right up through the netless rim and soared into the sky like a pop foul. With cool disdain, not so much as glancing at the awed crowd, he trotted down the court and waited for Timmie.

We worked the ball down but unexpectedly, Richie came up and aggressively held Timmie far outside and no matter how the kid wriggled and doodled and feinted and faked, he couldn't get in and even had trouble passing the ball off with Richie's arms surrounding him like a wraparound windshield. He finally got off a bounce pass but it was poor and Tatum stole it. Tatum looked up and there was Richie on the fast break, under our basket faster than a thought. Tatum hit him high with a baseball pass and in one motion he spun and stuffed the ball so hard you'd have thought it would shatter.

We tested Richie on defense again just to make sure the last time hadn't been a fluke. It hadn't been. He absolutely smothered Timmie and was so overwhelmingly big he blocked over picks as if they simply didn't exist. On one play, he slid off Timmie to guard me and I found myself enveloped in his shadow feeling like the hare who's just realized he's about to be an eagle's afternoon snack. I passed off to a teammate but now the rest of Richie's team was pumping adrenalin and they muffled us like a velvet curtain.

We started shooting—and missing—from the outside and rebound after rebound went to Richie. His team kept funneling the ball into him and he scored practically at will. It was a breathtaking display. Faking a broken shoelace, I called time out.

"That ain't no ballplayer," one of my teammates said shaking his head, "that's an act of God."

Mike Gilchrist, our captain, said, "We'll have to triple-team him."

"He'll just pass it off," I pointed out.

"No he won't," said Timmie.

"Why not?"

"Cause he out to prove somepin'."

I had to hand it to the kid. He had a lot of smarts.

"Let's try it," Mike said. "And on offense we just gotta keep shootin' from the outside—but sharper. And set up deeper picks, dig?"

I "repaired" my shoelace and we brought the ball down, trailing by a score of 17-14. I'd been having some luck, four baskets' worth, from the corners, and when the ball came to me I set up fast and dunked a jumper. We rushed down and Timmie, Mike, and I captured Richie in an unyielding pocket 15 or 20 feet from the basket. Now we'd see if Timmie's psychology worked.

Several of his teammates circled around him but he stubbornly held onto the ball and finally spun for a fade-away jump. It was amazing he got the shot off at all with thirty fingers waving in his eyes like a swarm of bees, but the ball came off the backboard sharply, we captured it and broke fast for a quick score.

Once again our triple defense contained Richie, who obstinately refused to pass off and kept trying to take it in himself. We stole the ball, brought it down, and set up a four-man alley for Timmie, who scored a honey of a layup to tie the score.

The strategy held and we battled to a 20-20 tie. The play became furious now and Richie, finally realizing his mistake, started passing off in a classical display of play-making but his teammates couldn't get off a decent shot.

Then we got a break. Tatum tried a long jumper. It bounded high off the rim and into my hands. I glanced down the court and found Timmie Lee rocketing toward the basket, two steps in front of Richie. I hurled the ball with all my might and hit Timmie perfectly. He veered in under the backboard for what seemed like an easy dunk. But suddenly and inexplicably he tripped and went sprawling into the crowd.

Rubbing a bleeding knee, he came back onto the court, sputtering. "You tripped me, man."

Richie put his hands on his hips and looked down at Timmie with open-mouthed astonishment. "I never touched you!"

Timmie smacked his palm with his fist. "You fuckin' tripped me, man, what you talkin' 'bout?"

"You tripped over your own shoes, man, don't blame me."

Timmie turned to the crowd and appealed. "He tripped me."

"He did, we saw it," they yelled. "He tripped him. The motherfucker tripped him."

"I haven't laid a finger on you all game," Richie said righteously.

"I don't give a shit what you done, faggot, you fuckin' tripped me."

We muscled in between them before they could come to blows. The argument continued and I pulled Richie aside. "Why don't we just take the play over?"

"No way," he said scornfully. "He tripped and it's our ball."

"Come on, son, winning isn't worth all these bad feelings."

"I can't help his bad feelings," Richie replied, tearing away from my grip and walking away.

The dispute raged on and neither party would compromise. Finally, I looked bleakly at Tatum and shrugged. He held up his hands in a what-are-you-gonna-do? gesture and that was that. The game ended in a bitterly controversial tie.

I felt I should say something to Timmie Lee but saw him talking to a smooth-looking black man dressed in a purple suit with a frilly shirt, broad-brimmed planter's hat, and platform shoes. He had a consoling arm around Timmie's shoulders and there was something in his proprietary air that made me uncomfortable, like watching a pimp strolling with his whore.

"Who's that, Tatum?"

"That's the cat I wanted to talk to you about, Dave. His name is Warnell Slakey and he's bad."

"I've heard that name."

"Probably so."

"What's his game?"

"He calls himself a college liaison representative or some shit like that."

I snapped my fingers. Slakey's name had come up several times in conversations with college coaches. He was one of a host of leeches who batten on the ignorance and inexperience of ghetto kids, in this case, their ambition to be basketball stars. The way he worked was first to insinuate himself into the graces of promising high school basketball players, slipping them money and doing them favors, speaking knowledgeably about college and pro sports, boasting of his intimate friendships with all the coaches, his familiarity with the deans who control scholarship money, his long list of basketball stars who had made it to college or the pros as a result of his string-pulling.

Probably 5 percent of this was true but the kids were invariably impressed and dazzled by his sharp clothes and big new car and they'd ask him to help them get introduced to coaches or scouts. Of course, he was delighted to—for a fee. One way or another, the kids would come up with the money—as often as not it was literally begged, borrowed, or stolen—and he'd then make a few phone calls. Occasionally, he really did convince a scout to come around for a look at his "client," and one thing would lead to another and the prospect would be offered a scholarship—on which Slakey would take a commission.

What the kids didn't realize was that sooner or later scouts would come around of their own accord anyway, since this is what they're paid to do. Or they'd follow up tips from high school coaches. If a kid was good enough, chances were, he'd be funneled onto the scholarship trail without the help of the Warnell Slakeys.

If Slakey were merely a parasite that would be bad enough but I'd heard worse about him, and Tatum confirmed it. "Motherfucker claims a commission on everything. Scouts come around to the schools, Slakey tells the kids *he* got him to come down and watch them play and makes them pay him a fee. A kids gets a scholarship, Slakey may not have lifted so much as a finger for him but puts the arm on him for a cut, claiming he swung the deal."

There was a word for it, extortion.

"How does he enforce the shakedowns?" I asked.

Tatum thrust his chin in the direction of a couple of muscular characters trailing Slakey and Timmie.

"Is Timmie into him for anything?"

"He's borrowed some money off of him," Tatum said, "but I don't think things have gone any further—yet. But I'm nervous, Dave. Slakey has a way of surrounding you till you're a captured man. And Slakey doesn't take kindly to kids who don't cooperate with him. He plays rough."

"Why don't you send Timmie around to see me?"

"I was hoping you'd say that."

He walked over to Richie, leaning dejectedly against a fence pole. "Sorry it ended this way, kid, but don't worry about it. These things happen. You played a helluva game. You're gonna be everything they say."

As they were shaking hands, Timmie Lee squirmed out of the protective arm of Slakey and strode across the court to where we were standing. We all tensed because the look in his eye was not one of brotherly love. Yet when he reached us he said to Richie, "I'm sorry, man."

I was uncertain what he was apologizing for but realized it wasn't as important as the fact that he had enough guts to say he was sorry. Richie took his hand, then put his arm around him. "I'll see you in the pros."

We crossed Seventh Avenue and caught the downtown bus. Richie, head and arms still glistening with sweat, sat with his hands clasped and his head bowed, looking out the window pensively at Central Park as we lumbered down 110th and turned onto Fifth Avenue. Every once in a while he would shake his head.

"Well," I said, "what do you think, Wings?"

"Fantastic. You know, Mr. Bolt, I'd take any five of

those guys and match them up with the college all-stars and give you even money. I'll bet they could even handle a few of the poorer pro teams."

"Probably not. They don't have the discipline. But one-on-one, some of them are as good as half the stars in the big leagues." I looked at Richie and got the feeling he was just making conversation. His eyes were staring far away and I sensed he was back on the court on 130th Street, replaying the incident that had broken up the game.

"Forget about it, son. It was just one of those things."

He gazed at me and opened and closed his mouth several times as if debating whether to say something to me. Finally, he said, *"You* don't think I tripped him, do you?"

"I didn't have a clear view. But that's not really the point anyway. The point, in *my* mind at least, is that you should have offered to do it over."

"I suppose you're right," he said, lapsing into another long silence. He was still brooding when we got off the bus at 56th Street. We walked to his hotel on 55th and lingered under the canopy. I felt he still had something he wanted to say. When at last he came out with it, it was with a shy, almost Cupid-like grin and he absolutely floored me. "I did trip him, you know."

I gaped. "Hit me again, podner?"

"I tripped him."

"But not on purpose!"

"Yes. On purpose."

"Good sweet Jesus, boy, what'd you go and do that for?"

"I had to stop him somehow," he replied ingenuously. "He was about to score the winning basket."

"But..."

"I just kicked his back foot into his front one. My father taught me that."

"But... but..." I could do nothing but stammer.

"He'd been cheap-shotting me all game long."

I felt a surge of indignation. "What the hell has that got to do with it? A foul is a foul. If he fouled you ten thousand times and you only fouled him once, yours is still a foul."

"I know, but—well, I'm not sure I can explain it. See, most of the time I can win on my own. I can afford . . . I can afford to be fair. I build up a reputation for fairness—establish credibility, you might say. But every once in a while, there's a situation—like today. When that happens, I draw on my credibility and everybody believes me." He grinned like a child.

"You mean, you build up cheating credits?"

A hurt look came into his eyes. "I call them honesty credits." He shrugged. "Everybody does it to some extent."

"True, true. I just didn't think you needed to, what with your gifts. I also didn't realize how badly you need to win."

"I've got to win," he said, and I thought I detected a cloud of little-boy fright pass across his face. I wondered at what point in his childhood triumph had become imperative. For some reason, I thought of his father.

Suddenly, and inexplicably, I laughed.

"What's so funny?"

It came to me. "Oh, I guess I'm relieved to know you're not a 100-percent saint." He smiled with me, a kind of Bambi smile that made him all the more likeable. I put my hand on his shoulder and thumped it. He wasn't the genuine article after all.

But he sure as shit was the closest thing to it.

CHAPTER III

• • • •

I only had to cool my heels for a minute in Niles Lauritzen's anteroom before Connie gave me the nod but it was a minute richly spent contemplating the nape of Connie's neck and assembling my thoughts for the meeting with her boss, the commissioner of the American Basketball Association.

Interestingly, I knew Connie's neck a lot more intimately than I knew her boss. It's an unwritten policy of mine to make friends with the secretaries of VIP's because secretaries hold the keys to such vital information as whether the boss is really down the hall taking a leak or actually avoiding speaking to you, or who he has in the conference room and how long they've been in there, or what's in the letter she just put in the mail to you. I don't always take them to bed, of course, even when they want to be taken, but in Connie's case, it had been the natural outcome of a rather steamy party thrown for Howard Cosell at the Playboy Club. Short and compact, redheaded and introverted, Connie could never have passed for a Playboy bunny but in bed, she was every keyholder's fantasy come true and we carried on like goats for a couple of weeks before a long business trip put a natural punctuation to the affair. We had remained flirting friends and now she was going with my best friend, Roy Lescade, a sportswriter for the *New York Post.*

The meeting with Lauritzen was not as pleasurable to think about, filled as it was with vast uncertainties but it promised, ultimately, far greater rewards. I had met the commissioner on several social occasions and we'd hobnobbed amicably but we'd had no real dealings and why should we have had? My business, essentially, was with the owners, not the league. And even at that moment, in the case of Richie Sadler, the logical thing would have been to approach not the commissioner but Stanley Vreel, owner of the ABA's Boston Bombers. But the stakes were not of the variety that dictated a logical approach, indeed, I was about to venture into a *terra incognita* whose topography defied logic. The only thing I had to guide me was the history of insanity in the negotiations over basketball stars' salaries in the last ten years.

I was determined to be perfectly sane.

With an ironically courteous nod to Connie, I shouldered open the door to Lauritzen's office and stepped into his intimidatingly spacious inner sanctum. It was decorated entirely in golds and reds, with ochre carpeting and tooled crimson leather seats, plush window hangings embroidered with fleurs-de-lis, and scrolled ormolu on everything but his Stenorette. Even the specially commissioned paintings of basketball scenes by Morton Kalish were done in reds and golds to fit in with the appointments. I felt like a clashing intrusion in my blue blazer and I ruminated that such discomfort might be deliberately planned by the commissioner to keep visitors off-balance. Lending credence to this notion, the commissioner himself was attired in a suit and tie so perfectly coordinated with the decor that it was hard to believe he hadn't brought a swatch of his carpet to his tailor.

I always felt a little odd in the presence of the commissioner anyway, simply because he was not the man you'd expect to find standing at the helm of a basketball federation. For one thing, he didn't give the impression he'd ever played the game. He couldn't have been more than 6-feet tall, was rather portly, and had the kind of doughy face you'd expect on a bank manager or shoe salesman. He also liked the distillate of corn mash more than a man in his position should, though he held his liquor well—and where I come from that's considered a higher virtue than patriotism. Nonetheless, despite appearances, he'd been an All-American at St. John's and put in a couple of high-scoring years in the 1930s with the New York Celtics before drifting into college coaching, front-office work, a public relations position with the NBA, and, ultimately, "czar" of the ABA. And also despite appearances, he was a damn good czar, too. In the four years of his administration, he'd managed to accomplish many things his predecessors had been unable to do, such as the imposition of the tightest clamp on pill-popping of any professional sport going. For that alone, you had to take your hat off to him.

"Hello Dave," he said, shaking my hand warmly and escorting me over to a gold-inlaid mahogany liquor cart.

"I think I'll pass if it's all right with you, sir."

He looked offended for a moment, then clapped a hand to his forehead. "Oh hell, I forgot," he said, looking embarrassed.

This was a reference to a segment of my life I'd just as soon forget, a two-year bat after my injury-forced retirement from football that is still, when I close my eyes and try to recall it, just a funky alcoholic haze filled with the blurry images of a wife and daughter and home and career all swept away in a river of bourbon.

"That's all right," I said. "It's just that at 10 in the morning, coffee has infinitely more appeal to me."

He buzzed Connie and ordered coffee for both of us. While we waited, Lauritzen asked, "Do you still like to be called 'Lightning'?"

I shrugged. "I lost the nickname when I got out of football but it seems to pop up now and then. I'm content with 'Dave.'"

"I also remember when they called you 'Sleeper.'"

I grinned. "That goes back some, to Fort Worth High. They dubbed me that because I was always surprising the opposition. I was just a shrimp then but I could burn 'em. I'd have kept the name too but after graduation I started growing again, mostly in the arms and legs department. By the time I got to college there wasn't any way I could pass for a sleeper."

Connie brought in a silver coffee service. It flashed so brightly I had difficulty making out the rosy swells of her breasts as she stooped over in her low-cut blouse and placed the tray on the coffee table.

"Of course," I said, stirring a spoonful of sugar into my cup and looking meaningfully at Lauritzen, "I'm still something of a sleeper in a few ways."

"So I've been told."

That got my curiosity up. "People think I'm worth talking about, do they?"

"Don't sell yourself short. You're considered one of the better agents in the field, Dave. The only person you don't promote aggressively enough is yourself."

"I come from plains settlers, Mr. Lauritzen. High visibility was considered bad form. Folks that stuck their heads up too high usually caught a Comanche arrow in the eye. My daddy told me to keep my head down and my pecker up—and that seems to have carried me through life pretty well."

The commissioner brushed a silver sideburn with his index finger. "How does that apply to Richie Sadler's career?"

"Ah, you know what I'm here for, then?"

"It wasn't hard to guess. You were seen at Maxwell's Plum with Richie on Friday night—or don't you read Earl Wilson's column? —and you call me first thing Monday morning to make an appointment with me second thing Monday morning. My only question is, what do you want with *me?* Your business is with Stanley Vreel up in Boston. He drafted Richie and it's his money, if he wants to spend it."

"No, you're my main man, sir. It's all going to come back to you anyway because the price I'm asking can't possibly be met by one club. In fact, I'm not sure it can be met by one nation."

He smiled nervously. "But Richie *does* want to go with the ABA?"

"Naturally, I'm going to have to sound the NBA out too and if they offer a billion dollars, I suppose I'll have to consider it. But Richie really does want to go with the ABA, if you can meet his terms."

His nervous smile became a nervous laugh. "Well at least I know you're asking less than a billion dollars."

He sipped his coffee silently and appeared to have sent his mind down the road a mile or two to guess what I was going to ask and how he was going to react. Then he dabbed at his mouth with a delicate linen napkin and said, "It would be silly for me to deny that the ABA wants Richie Sadler and wants him very badly. I think he could open the door to big television money, and beyond that, to merger. It would also be foolish for me to tell you we're not prepared to subsidize his purchase by the Boston Bombers. But you have to understand that the league is not fundamentally a bank, and certainly not a gold mine.

To subsidize any deal with Richie Sadler, I have to assess the other ABA owners and they've been squeezed hard already by some other player acquisitions. So ..."

Lauritzen picked up a bronze paperweight that looked like, and probably was, an Olympic medal. "So, what kind of figure are we talking about?"

And now a strange thing happened. I'd rehearsed it in my mind all weekend. In my imagination, I tossed the figure on the table as effortlessly as if it were petty cash. But now that it was time to say the damn thing out loud, I choked. I don't think I've been so uptight since my first regular season game as a Dallas Cowboy, when on my first pattern, I forgot to look in on a look-in and the pass hit me spang on the left buttock.

"Well," I drawled, "there are a number of rather complicated devices aimed at amortizing the principal and reducing net taxable income and I'm omitting for the sake of simplicity some fringe items such as a car and a home, which we can take up later. Then in addition, there are such considerations as subsidiary rights... "

Lauritzen cleared his throat and my voice trailed off. "Dave, you're a plain-talking man from Texas and I'm a plain-talking man from Queens, right?"

"Yes sir."

"Well then, suppose you drop all this bullshit and just tell me what the bottom line is."

I felt my cheeks redden. "You're right, commissioner, I've been beating around the bush. But then, I've never been involved in a bush anywhere near this big."

"I promise you, I won't have a coronary."

I took a deep breath and exhaled it slowly. "Three million."

If he flinched, I didn't see it. He simply looked out the window, then turned and said, "For how long, thirty years?"

But to assure me that this was just a joke, he allowed something resembling a smile to trickle out of the corners of his mouth. A big contract did not look quite so imposing if it covered a long period. Julius Erving, a few years back, had signed a contract for over four million bucks but some of that was an indemnity to a team he'd previously played for, and the rest covered an eight-year contract.

"No," I said. "Two." My heart was pounding furiously and my fingernails biting into the impeccable upholstery of my chair. Despite four spoonsful of sugar in my coffee, my mouth was so dry I couldn't manufacture enough spit to make a postage stamp stick.

"Three million dollars for a two-year contract," Lauritzen repeated tonelessly. "How do you want that—in fives and tens?"

"A million-dollar bonus and the rest in salary, payable in convenient installments."

"Can you think of a convenient way to pay out three million dollars?" Lauritzen asked. I think he had to keep joking to keep the enormity of the demand from crushing him.

"Look at it this way, commissioner. The box-office appeal of a million-dollar bonus baby will be irresistible. People who don't know a hoop from a brass ring are going to swarm to the arenas out of sheer curiosity. Look at what happened when the Jets paid Joe Namath a $400,000 bonus. It was the biggest hype the American Football League ever pulled off. It led demonstrably to merger with the NFL. Now, I can't swear Richie will do the same thing for basketball but you know how close we are now. The television networks are leaning against the door, commissioner, all it's gonna take is Richie Sadler to open it and they'll come tumbling in around your feet."

Lauritzen started to argue but I poured it on. "Another

thing. With the merger of the two major basketball leagues, the salary war will come to a halt. You'll easily make up the money paid for Richie with savings on all those other salaries and reductions of bonuses when things stabilize. You'll be putting millions back in the pockets of the owners. Not that I think *that's* such a terrific notion, mind you..."

"You're very glib, Dave, but you're not facing the owners and telling them they're going to be assessed several hundred thousand dollars apiece to pay for this *Wunderkind*. I'll be lucky if I escape with my scalp intact. Is there at least a little 'give' in your price? Something negotiable I can hold out to the owners?"

"Uh-uh," I said. "The only 'give' is Richie's 'take'—three million skins. The negotiable area is how the money will be paid out."

Lauritzen leaned heavily against the wall and shook his head like a bear. "There's only one way the money can be paid out, Dave."

"How's that?"

"Painfully."

CHAPTER IV

• • • •

I had just enough time after the meeting with Commissioner Lauritzen to taxi out to La Guardia Airport and catch the noon Eastern Airlines shuttle up to Boston. I took a bus into midtown Boston, then taxied over to Beacon Street where Stanley Vreel's corporate offices were located. I had boned up on Vreel, the owner of the Boston Bombers, but somehow my mental picture of him was still two-dimensional. Apparently, others had experienced this problem too. Despite an extroverted personality and a love of publicity, he was something of a mystery. A former Bronx boy, he was a self-made millionaire who'd called all the right investment shots in the booming fifties, then shrewdly had gotten out of the stock market just before the invasion of the bears. There was some talk of his having manipulated some issues in a way that brought the SEC sniffing around his door. Rumors like that never surprise me; I hold with Balzac who said that behind every fortune there is a crime. Anyway, the SEC investigation blew over.

When he pulled out of the stock market in the sixties, Vreel cannily judged that the coming thing was leisure and began pushing his chips over to things like marinas, golf courses, and sports stadiums. You'd think he'd have made a killing but from all accounts—and I'd checked into these with the thoroughness of a CPA—he was more like the killee. It seems that between the money crunch and rising labor costs, he'd barely broken even and then when the energy crisis came to a head, crimping the leisure industry like a dull axe, Vreel really took a bath. Now he was just another of your cash-poor, hard-working millionaires.

One of his brainstorms, before he got creamed by those same wonderful economic forces that brought you the recession, had been to start a second basketball franchise in Boston, fielding an ABA team that would compete for gate revenue with the NBA's complacent Celtics. Considering that his first team was comprised of misfits, callow rookies, geriatric cases, and NBA retreads, Vreel had managed to attract crowds with pure gaudy ballsy showmanship and lost only $100,000 on the Bombers in their first year.

Vreel was a little Napoleon type, short and bristling with nervous energy. An excellent and fastidious dresser, he reminded me of Hank Stram, coach of the Kansas City Chiefs, even down to the rolled-up magazine he banged against his thigh as he paced up and down his office listening to my terms for Richie Sadler. But whereas Commissioner Lauritzen had received them with the sad-eyed resignation of a virgin about to be gang-banged, Vreel waxed absolutely apoplectic.

"You know something, Bolt," he said in an ominously quiet tone, like a mountainful of bubbling magma looking for a fissure, "it's fucks like you that are ruining professional sports."

I'd been called worse names and wasn't particularly upset. My daddy told me to put myself in the other guy's britches and imagine how he feels—in this case, how he feels about being asked to fork up a bushel of money to cover an investment of four or five million dollars that wasn't even making money. I just held my tongue and rode out the storm of Vreel's indignation.

It was one of your better storms of indignation. He marched out every classical argument about how basketball used to be wholesome and unsullied until the parasites swarmed over it, and how outrageous salary demands were forcing owners into inflationary spirals that ended with higher ticket prices for the poor man in the street, and how the flower of American youth was being corrupted by easy money. The least excoriating epithet he used on me was "buccaneer," but I also was a target for four "cocksuckers," two "fuckfaces," two "shitasses," and even a "cunt."

When he'd wound down a bit, he said, "Look, Bolt, this may sound hard to believe, but I don't have that kind of money."

"I have some pals on Wall Street who told me you do."

"It's all on paper, for Christ's sake."

"Convert it," I said pleasantly.

"I can, at a terrible loss. Or don't you follow the financial pages?"

"But I told you, the league is going to subsidize you. The commissioner's out right now rounding up pledges."

"How much do you think he can round up, for crying out loud?" Vreel exploded. "Don't you think the other owners have troubles of their own?"

I went into the same number with him that I'd gone into with the commissioner, but somehow, all my airy promises that a golden age of basketball was near at hand couldn't offset the concrete reality of the price I was asking for Richie Sadler. With a wild wave of the hand he said, "All right, all right, all right, you've made your point. Now get outta here, I got to count my money. I'll call you in a couple of days."

I didn't bother offering my hand since I was certain he wouldn't shake it but just as I was reaching for the doorknob he called out to me.

"Bolt? Come here."

I walked back slowly and he put his index finger on my lapel. "Bolt, what do you really want?" His eyes were black and piercing and hypnotic and made me uncomfortable, as if they could penetrate to that pocket of larceny that, as the saying goes, there's a little bit of in every man.

"What do I really want?" I repeated, not quite getting his drift. "I told you what I want. Three mil—"

"No, no. I mean for yourself."

"For myself? Why, 10 percent of... ah. *Ah!*"

Lights went off in my head. He was sounding me out, in essence, about a kickback for me if I would lower my demands. The proposition was simple enough and far more common than some of my colleagues would like to admit. It works this way: I drop the price for Richie from three million dollars to, say, one, for which Vreel pays me under the table, oh, say $400,000. So he gets Richie for a total of $1.4 million instead of three, and I end up not with $300,000—10 percent of Richie's three-million-dollar contract but $500,000: Vreel's $400,000 kickback plus 10 percent of Richie's million-dollar contract.

There *is* a little bit of larcenist in me, but for practical as well as moral reasons, I draw the line at selling a client down the river. As he ushered me to the door, I'd already made my decision but I thought it best to let him think there was a chance I'd go for the scheme. "Tell you what, Mr. Vreel. I'll think it over. But I want *you* to think over what you're going to do if I decide I don't want anything 'for myself.'"

"Fair enough, but I believe that if you think about it, you'll see how advantageous my counter-proposal could be." This time he shook my hand. "Whenever you're ready, I'll be glad to fly down to New York, okay?"

"Sure."

"I'll have my chauffeur drive you to the airport." Although we were not yet prepared to consider the NBA seriously, it was only sound business practice to cover my bets in the event my negotiations with the ABA broke down. So in the next couple of days, I conferred with Sam Fine, commissioner of the NBA, and with Hy Tishoff, owner of the NBA's Newark Nationals, the other expansion team that had drafted Richie. These sessions were slightly less turbulent than the North Atlantic during the hurricane season and I concluded at the end of them that if you really want to be liked, you shouldn't be an agent.

But there was no danger of my being liked, believe me. Commissioner Fine threw me out of his office, and Tishoff became completely hysterical and incoherent and warned me he had the power to ruin Richie by smearing him with a story about underworld associations. That's when I finally lost my cool. I'd been getting nothing but grief all week and now I was being threatened by this tubby little prick whose own criminal associations were so thick you could almost see the puppeteer's strings working his arms and legs. I hauled him off the floor and said, "Mr. Tishoff, the day Richie Sadler plays for the Newark Nationals, I will kiss your ass in Madison Square Garden for a half-time ceremony."

Owners are wonderful. Give me a roomful of them or a pit full of rattlesnakes and I'll take my chances with the rattlers any day of the week.

After a few days, things began to shake out. Big salary deals make sensational headlines, but the details of negotiation make dull reading, so I'll gloss over them. Commissioner Lauritzen went not to the owners first but to

Roone Arledge, ABC-TV's sports programming genius, and managed to get something a little less than a commitment but more than a promise that Arledge would push for his network's pickup of ABA basketball the following season if Richie Sadler became a Boston Bomber. Now, with something of a mandate, Commissioner Lauritzen could feel a little easier about hitting up the other ABA owners for an assessment to cover the cost of Richie Sadler. The groans were audible as far off as Rangoon but by the beginning of the following week, we were just about home.

I then informed my friend Vreel up in Boston that I wasn't interested in his "counterproposal," and gave him a couple of days to fall into line. This he did on Wednesday, kicking and screaming all the way. There ensued two more days of intensely boring meetings with Vreel and Commissioner Lauritzen working out innumerable details. On Friday, we signed a short letter of agreement covering the broader contours of our understanding preparatory to inking, as the sports columnists love to say, the formal pact. That night we threw a party to announce the deal.

I'd asked Davis Sadler and Richie to remain in town for consultation and they in turn had prevailed on Mrs. Sadler and Sondra to stay on and make a vacation out of it. Their holiday reached a crashing finale in this combined press conference and celebratory bash in the cavernous office of Commissioner Lauritzen. There were journalists galore, a clutch of sports stars, and grinning brass from both basketball leagues, and we posed for pictures of Richie signing the agreement, accepting a down-payment check, the usual horseshit. Arledge and some ABC flunkies showed up but preferred not to pose just yet for any pictures. Howard Cosell, on the other hand, had no such reservations. I came as close to getting snockered as I'd been since my two-year toot ten years earlier, but I forgave myself. How often do you swing one of the biggest deals in basketball history?

There was only one sad face at the party and it belonged to Sondra Sadler. You can't win 'em all, of course, but it bugged me to see that haunting mouth contorted with unhappiness. I tried to get a word with her but she kept slipping into the crowd to avoid me. At last, I cornered her near the trophy case. "Goddam, you're harder to catch than a loon on a lake." She tried to pull away but I put a firm hand on her arm. "Come on, darlin', won't you suspend hostilities with me for just an hour?"

She looked out at the laughing throng bathed in a miasma of cigar smoke. "Am I supposed to love this? I think it's disgusting!"

"Hey, listen here. Fame doesn't destroy everybody—just those who have self-destruction inside them to begin with. I don't think your brother is one of them, probably thanks to you. So, what do you say to a smile?"

"What's there to smile about?"

"Well... there's the one about the woman acrobat who was torn between two strongmen."

It caught her off guard and she emitted a tinkling little laugh.

"Don't you laugh now," I teased, "don't you dare laugh."

She laughed harder and I joined in.

It was the last good laugh we were to have together for some time.

CHAPTER V

• • • •

Trish stuck her head in the door. "It's Sondra on 40."

"I guess she wants to say goodbye. Hey, you all right?"

"A little punchy and slightly sick and tired of your unshaven face. Otherwise, fine."

We'd spent the weekend cooped up in the office drafting the final formal agreements on the Richie Sadler deal. The work had been just short of murderous. "Well," I said, handing her an envelope, "maybe this'll make up for it."

She squinted at me and opened it with a frown. Then her eyes rounded in delight as she took out the check. "What's this for?"

"Bonus. For taking Sondra and her mother around. You did as much in your way to swing this deal—no, no, don't argue with me. It's hard to find your kind of hospitality outside of the South."

"Shit, Dave." She looked genuinely embarrassed.

"Anyway, do me two favors. Don't deposit the check for a few days until Vreel's binder clears."

"Sure. And what's the other?"

"Don't call me a *bubby*. I hate that word!"

She leaned over and kissed me on the ear. "You really are a *bubby.*"

I felt a funny sort of gladness as I said hello to Sondra. As fiendishly hard as I'd worked all weekend, the image of Richie's sister laughing had never been far from my mind's eye and came shimmering forth radiantly whenever I took a break. I don't know what it was. We'd talked for only a few minutes more at the party and it had been strictly informational. She told me she was an artist, that her hobby was horseback riding, that she hoped to get married one day and live on a farm and paint and have three children, preferably boys. It was just about as interesting as the 5-second précis quiz-show contestants give the home audience so why I should find it so fascinating was a mystery to me. She had expressed no reciprocal interest in my life story which rankled within me for reasons I couldn't explain. Well, yes I could. I guess if she hadn't been going home that day... oh, what the hell.

"Is Richie with you?" she asked without salutation.

"No, is he supposed to be?"

"He didn't say."

"When did he go out?"

"Last evening."

"Last *evening?* You mean he's been gone since then?"

"Yes."

I felt a slight tremor of anxiety but we still had a long way to go before pushing the panic button. "Where was he going last evening?"

"Nowhere, at least not that he mentioned. He just excused himself after dinner and said he was going out for a while."

"Ah," I laughed. *"Cherchez la femme.* He probably met someone and is conducting what my people like to call a dalliance."

"He'd have called. He isn't shy about telling us he's spending the night with someone."

"I still wouldn't be concerned," I said, concerned. "When is your flight?"

"This evening at 8."

"He'll show up, you'll see. What do your folks say?"

"Oh, they think he's—um, shacked up too."

"There you go. Not to worry." I drummed the desk. "Tell you what. If you don't hear from Richie by noon, why don't you drop up to the office and we'll make some phone calls."

I plunged into a pile of work I'd neglected the last week, as much for therapy as anything else. Like barbarians at the walls of Rome, a host of disquieting fantasies were shouldering the gates of my normal tranquility, and only the distraction of hard work kept them out. Every time the phone rang I jumped, expecting Lord knows what, perhaps the city morgue asking me if I had a client whose feet extended half a yard over the end of a standard coroner's slab, or Sondra reporting that Richie had just ambled into the hotel with a shit-eating grin, reeking of perfume and graffitied with lipstick. But no such calls came in. What did come in, at 12:30, was Sondra herself—and that's when I got my first attack of the scaries.

One thing I had to say for her, she was a good dresser. Unlike most of your Midwestern gals, she followed the fashion magazines and wasn't two years behind the times or even two minutes. She was wearing a brown denim pantsuit over a ribbed T-shirt, Italian sandals and the latest bangles and she could have been a native New York chick out on her lunch hour. I liked that, most of the time they come in from St. Louis or Kansas City wearing those nubby white linen suits, white shoes and pillbox hats.

What I didn't like about Sondra was her expression. She'd obviously been biting her lip all morning for there was a sore in the corner, her eyes were puffy with sleeplessness, and their look was one of distress bordering on fear.

It was infectious but I waved casually and fought to keep a lid on my own nervousness. "Still no sign of our bonus baby?"

"No."

"The girl must be good."

"I'm telling you, he's not with any girl. Something's happened to him."

"We'd have heard by now."

"Not necessarily. He could have been mugged and stripped of all his identification cards."

"I doubt it," I said. "In the first place, most muggers can't reach high enough to hit your brother on the head. And in the second, Richie isn't that hard to identify when you get right down to it."

This time there was no making her laugh. "I don't think you're taking this very seriously, Mr. Bolt. I'd have thought that if for no other reason than to protect your commission..."

"Ouch, that's a low blow, honey! It's just that I'm not going to be stampeded. New York City is the biggest fleshpot in the world and I've seen some pretty God-fearing boys go wild once they got here. And your brother's got more reason than most to take himself on a lost weekend, what with the way he's been hounded by the press and all."

"You said you'd make some phone calls."

"I did but I'm a little reluctant about it for the moment. It might only upset a lot of people unduly, generate some lurid publicity, and spatter egg on our faces when Richie walks in and says he's simply been locked in the arms of a particularly possessive sports groupie. So I think we should wait a few hours more... Have you had lunch yet?"

"No, and I'm not hungry."

"A person's got to eat."

"A person's got to smoke." She surveyed the littered top of my desk until she found a cigarette box.

I struck a match for her. "I didn't know you smoked."

"I do, under stress."

"There must be something less destructive you can do under stress."

She sucked in a big lungful of smoke. "I look at pictures."

"I have a print of *Deep Throat* back at my apartment."

She glared at me. "Why do you feel so compelled to try to make me laugh?"

"Why do you feel so compelled to frown?"

She inhaled again. "By pictures I meant paintings."

"You're in the right city for paintings."

"I've been to just about every museum in New York since we got here."

"Some of our best art isn't in museums. You like Kandinsky?"

She looked at me with contempt. "What do *you* know about Kandinsky?"

That ticked me off. "Believe it or not, there's some folks from Texas who know more about the world than roping steers."

She pressed her knuckles to her brow. "I'm sorry, that was stupid of me. I don't know what I'm saying today."

"Just say you'd like to see some Kandinskys most people don't know about."

"Yes, I would, if..."

I buzzed Trish. "Call Morty Tepper and ask him if I can bring someone over to see his collection."

"Who's Morty Tepper?" Sondra asked.

"He owns a large piece of the New York Nets. And he's a collector. Picks up painters when they're cheap, same as he does basketball players."

Trish buzzed back and told me Morty had said it would be fine, his wife would be home to show us around the gallery.

Sondra hesitated. "What if...?"

"Don't worry." I instructed Trish to phone us at Morty's the second she heard from Richie.

We left the Lincoln Building on the 42nd Street side, crossed the street and got a cab easily in front of Grand Central Station. I told the driver to take Sixth Avenue, then head north through Central Park.

The park was resplendent in the deepening green of maturing leaves and the warmth of a shimmering May morning had brought out throngs of lovers, softball players, mothers and toddlers, kids and dogs. I looked at Sondra and was gratified to see the tension in her face start to fade.

"Do you like Kandinsky?" she asked, studying my face with interest for the first time.

"He's a little too subtle for me. I like flashier stuff. Like Vasarely."

She greeted this with a mixture of distaste for Vasarely and surprise that I had any opinion at all.

"Are you seriously interested in art?"

"I would be if I had more time. Still, I've managed to pick up some opinions here and there. Same goes for books and music. My problem is, most of the people I deal with are athletes—athletes and what you might call athletic supporters—owners and agents and sportswriters."

She made a wry face at the pun.

"Anyway, with all these jock types around," I continued, "I don't get much of a chance to talk about anything besides sports—except maybe women."

"You study women?" Though she was still boycotting smiles, there was amusement in her eyes.

"I try to make time for that." I hesitated, then said, "I've been studying you, a little."

"Me? I'm a short course. A half hour and you know everything."

"I think there's a lot more than that."

She shifted on her seat. "What has your study revealed?"

"Aside from how beautiful you are, you mean?"

"Mr. Bolt..."

"Okay, okay, I'm sorry. I really meant ugly."

"Why don't you stop trying to be the chivalrous southerner and just say what you mean."

"Okay, then. I would say your guiding character trait is responsibility," I said.

Her eyebrows raised and I could see I'd struck close to home.

"In fact, I'd say you sometimes wish you weren't so responsible."

"You're a good student, Mr. Bolt."

"You wouldn't want to drop the 'Mr. Bolt' routine would you?"

She looked out the window, apparently, thinking it over carefully as if it were a major decision. And perhaps it was, for when she turned back she said, "Not yet, if you don't mind."

"Suit yourself," I shrugged.

"And what's *your* guiding trait?" she asked.

"You haven't been studying me?" I said it mockingly but I really was disappointed at her aloofness.

"I wouldn't say studying, but I have observed you, I suppose."

"And what's your observation?"

"Mmm—that you may be a little more complex than I thought." She looked at me and hastily added, "Now, don't look so smug. Anyone who prefers Vasarely to Kandinsky is not *that* complex."

"You sure do give up ground grudgingly," I said.

We exited the park at 90th Street, swung right at Fifth Avenue and then left at 88th Street. The cab pulled up beside a turreted mansion of smudged marble, decorated with gargoyles and seraphim and saints and prophets. I ran down the building's history for Sondra—it originally had been built by the Schupfs of diamond fame and was now an official landmark—and rang the bell.

Morty's wife Suzanne, a dark, vivacious, and thoroughly unpretentious woman greeted us warmly. We chatted for a few minutes over tea and finger sandwiches that she had thoughtfully prepared in advance. Then she escorted us to the gallery and left us on our own.

We strolled through it at a leisurely pace, and Sondra really began to open up, discoursing authoritatively out of what was, apparently, an astonishing store of information. Her face became animated and she gestured gracefully with flowing hands and fingers, helping me visualize the artists' conceptions and judge how well those conceptions had been translated onto canvas.

We stopped before a large Kandinsky, and after expatiating on the significance of the three shaded brown squares in a medium of yellow—which without Sondra's interpretation would have been little more to me than three shaded brown squares in a medium of yellow—she said, "Do you still prefer Vasarely?"

"Vasarely?" I sneered. "That cheap magician?"

She touched my arm. "You certainly make your mind up fast!"

"About certain things, I do." I gazed at her and held her eyes for a deliciously long moment.

"Dave..."

She brought the curtain down again over her eyes, as

she'd done in the cab. But this time, I had reason to feel encouraged. She'd unwittingly called me by my first name.

I was about to bring this to her attention when the gallery door opened. It was Suzanne Tepper. "Dave? Your office just called."

We both stiffened. For a few minutes, we'd forgotten about Richie. Now we were seized with apprehension. "What did my secretary say?"

Suzanne handed me a slip of paper on which she'd jotted down Trish's message in a scrupulous hand. "You're to call Niles Lauritzen right away at this number."

"She didn't say anything more?" Sondra asked her.

"Only that the commissioner said it was urgent."

Suzanne led us to a room off the gallery that served as an office. There was a desk with a telephone. I sat down and dialed the commissioner's number. Sondra stood over me, her hand resting heavily on my shoulder for support. I pointed to a chair in the corner but she didn't want to sit.

Connie put me right through to the commissioner and his voice trembled when he said hello. A surge of fear swept through my stomach. "Dave, you'd better get down here right away."

"Is this about Richie?"

"Yes."

"What's happened?"

"I'd rather not talk about it on the phone. Just get down here."

"Is he all right? Can you at least tell me that?"

"Dave, will you just get the hell down here?"

"Right."

I looked at Sondra. Her face was white and she was biting the back of her hand. I can't imagine I looked any less terrified.

CHAPTER VI

....

As the taxi inched maddeningly through the institutionalized traffic jam that is the intersection of Fifth Avenue and 57th Street, I pleaded with Sondra to let me drop her off at her hotel or even at my office, where she would have her parents or Trish to hold her hand until I could phone in the news. But she refused and slid out of the cab with me when we pulled up before 666 Fifth Avenue's aluminum facade.

The commissioner came out of his office to greet me personally when Connie buzzed him on the intercom but scowled when he saw Sondra and raised his hand before she could speak. He pulled us into a carpeted corridor and said, "I don't want Connie or anybody else to know something's wrong."

"What *is* wrong?" Sondra shot at him. "What's the matter with Richie?"

He grimaced and looked at me. "Did you have to bring her?"

"She was with me when I called you from Morty Tepper's." He shook his head as if this created a bothersome complication and I added, "She *is* his sister, commissioner."

He gestured toward his office and ushered us in. I wrinkled my nose at the odor of stale cigar smoke still clinging to the walls three days after the party.

A short, solid man in a tailored dark suit stood by the windows with his back to me, pounding his thigh with his fist. He turned when we came in. It was Stanley Vreel. His grave face lengthened when he saw Sondra. "She insisted on coming in," Commissioner Lauritzen explained.

"Great! That's all we need!" Vreel snorted. "Why don't I just call *Time?* Maybe we can make the cover."

Sondra's body tensed but I cut her off before she could retort. "Why don't you tell us what this is all about?"

Lauritzen and Vreel looked at each other and their eyes finally conceded there was no way short of main force to remove Sondra from the room.

"Your brother seems to have been uh, abducted."

"Abducted? Kidnapped?" she gasped rocking on her feet. I tried to ease her into a chair but she pushed me away.

"Kidnapped, abducted, what the hell difference does it make what you call it?" Vreel snarled, tugging at the knot in his tie and pacing like a caged puma from trophy case to the windows and back to the trophy case.

The commissioner picked up a shot glass of bourbon sitting on the coffee table and chugged it neat down his throat, then went over to the bar and refilled it.

"What exactly happened?" I asked accepting his offer of a glass for myself.

It was Vreel who answered. "I was packing to return to Boston with the contracts. That was a little more than an hour ago, a few minutes after 2, at the Plaza. The phone rang and it was this man telling me he was holding Richie a prisoner."

"What did he sound like?" I asked. "What exactly did he say?"

"His voice was kind of a deep baritone, a little gravelly,

no one I've ever spoken to before, I don't think. His exact words were, 'I've got Richie Sadler. If you want him back, you'll have to pay for him.' "

"You told me it was, 'If you want him back *alive,* you'll have to pay for him,'" the commissioner corrected him.

"I was only trying to spare Miss Sadler's feelings," Vreel said.

Sondra was swaying. "Did he say Richie was all right?"

"He actually let me speak to him," Vreel said. "He sounded fine, a little nervous. He said, 'Tell my folks and my sister I'm okay but please get me out of here. These men aren't fooling around.' "

"You're sure he said, 'These men'?"

"Yes, I'm quite sure. Then I said to him, 'Can you give me a hint about where you are?' But the other voice interrupted me. The guy said, 'I'm on the extension, so forget about that shit.'"

"Did it sound like a long-distance call?" I asked.

"No, but not really local either. There was some crackle."

"You mean, like it could have been coming from Long Island or Westchester or somewhere like that?" I said.

"Yes, but that still covers a lot of territory," Vreel answered. "Anyway, I said to the man, 'What do you want?' He said, 'What do you think we want, pal?' I said, 'All right, then, how much?'"

Apparently, we were coming to the hard part. Vreel went to the bar and fixed himself a tall, undiluted scotch and sipped it morosely. Our eyes followed his every move, as though there would be some clue in one of his motions.

"Well?" Sondra finally snapped. "How much?"

Vreel pounded his thigh once again. "The, uh, the man said to me, 'The newspapers say the kid is worth three million. Fine. We'll take three million.' "

Sondra looked shaky so I helped her to a chair. I was none too steady myself. The commissioner just mumbled the figure aloud. Vreel looked at his shoes.

"What'd you say to him?" I asked.

"I said, 'Come on now, be reasonable,' but he said, 'I'll give you a couple of days to round up the money, then I'll call you back with instructions.' "

"That's all he said?" Sondra asked, starting to cry.

"Tell them the last thing he said to you," the commissioner prompted Vreel.

"Oh yes. He said, 'I've seen the same movies you have, so don't try any tricks.'"

We all looked at Sondra. As if cut off by a spigot, the tears had stopped streaming down her face and she seemed strangely composed as if the only thing she'd heard in all this was that Richie was safe. I'm no psychologist but I think she must have been in some kind of shock, for, as casually as you might ask a soda jerk for a fudge sundae, she said to the commissioner, "Three million dollars shouldn't be that hard to raise, should it?" The commissioner's bugged-out eyes were almost funny to behold. Vreel had stopped pacing mid-step and was standing like a flamingo with one leg hovering over the carpet, trying to make sense of what he'd heard.

I gave them a sign and said to Sondra, "Well, we don't exactly have that sum readily available but it shouldn't be too hard to raise. Now, I'm going to have Trish come around and take you back to the hotel. We're going to discuss strategy and I'll join you just as soon as we've talked this thing over."

We sat Sondra down in a little waiting room with a television set and turned on some mindless serial while I phoned Trish and told her to haul her ass over here faster than a bullet in flight. She made it in 10 minutes. I briefed her, swore her to secrecy and instructed her as to how to handle Mr. and Mrs. Sadler till I could get there. Then we helped Sondra out of the office. She still had that blank look in her eyes and that disturbingly placid smile on her mouth. She'd freaked and it was probably the best thing that could have happened to her. My own circuits were pretty close to overloaded themselves.

Then we returned to the commissioner's office. "Did you call the FBI?" I asked him.

"No."

"But you plan to?"

"No."

"No?"

"Not yet. Stanley doesn't think we should. I tend to agree."

"But—hell, isn't that a crime too, not reporting a crime? I think that makes us accomplices after the fact or something."

"I know what it makes us!" Lauritzen barked. Then he looked at me remorsefully. "I'm sorry, Dave."

"It's all right, commissioner. You're in a helluva spot."

"Look," he said after another refueling at the bar, "here's our reasoning. We bring in the FBI, they're going to have to go after these people. And if they do they just may pull some damnfool stunt that'll backfire."

"They're very competent people, commissioner."

"They fuck up like anybody else. And it scares the hell out of me, what could happen if they fuck up. But that's not all."

"There's the publicity," Vreel said, resuming his pacing. "The press gets a hold of this story, they're gonna make a goddamn circus out of it. They'll only complicate our efforts and maybe destroy any chance we have of getting Richie back alive. And something else I've been thinking, you publicize this kidnapping and I guarantee every other sports star in the country will become fair game for nuts like these. Instead of hijacking planes, the new national pastime will be snatching ballplayers for ransom. We've got to keep a lid on this thing, at least until we've exhausted our own resources."

They looked at me. "You've got to make it unanimous, Dave."

I wasn't ready to put my career on the line just yet, to say anything of risking a jail sentence. "What do you mean by 'our own resources', Vreel?"

He looked at the commissioner, who said, "I have my own 'FBI.' "

For a moment I didn't understand. Then I remembered. Although they appear nowhere on the league's official payroll, except maybe as "advisers" or "consultants", the commissioner employed a squad of operatives to investigate the sort of activities that professional sports like to keep "in the family": gambling, drug abuse, underworld connections, sex scandals, that sort of thing. I'd heard about these gray eminences and since then have learned that every league employs them, though the brass usually deny it and disavow anyone who claims to be one. I've often wondered if my own humidor or the picture of Aunt Gussie on my dresser was bugged. Not that I have that much to hide except maybe from Internal Revenue.

The commissioner suggested we call in this investigative unit, composed mainly of retired basketball players, to dope out a scheme for tracking down and possibly trapping the kidnappers. We hashed out a lot of possible plans for another half hour or so then lapsed into troubled silence. The most important consideration of all hung unspoken in the air. Vreel waited for it like a convict with a noose around his neck, the commissioner like a reluctant hangman. That left it for me to broach it.

"Uh, what about the money, boys?"

There was a lot of squirming, heavy breathing, tapping of fingers on tables, and clacking of tongues on dry palates.

"To refresh your memories, they want three million dollars for Richie Sadler," I said. "My impression is that they will not accept three Jerry Wests, four Jim McMillians, and a Willis Reed."

The commissioner cleared his throat. "I've been thinking about that."

"I reckon you have," I said.

Vreel shrugged. "Well, we're not going to pay, that's all."

The declaration was greeted by an embarrassed silence. Suddenly Vreel's face darkened. "Commissioner, you're not thinking... why, that's... that's... unthinkable!"

The commissioner looked into his bourbon glass for support. "You're not thinking logically, Stanley. We've been beating all around the bush but we haven't considered the worst possibility. Suppose these guys are pros, suppose they've thought of every contingency, suppose in the end they outsmart us. Suppose, in other words, that our efforts to find Richie and get him back fail. Where does that leave us? I'll tell you where. It leaves us paying three million dollars for him."

"Maybe that's where it leaves *you*," Vreel said, lighting a cigar, "but it's not where it leaves me." He was bathed in a cloud of blue smoke for half a minute and when it thinned he said, "Richie Sadler may be worth three million dollars once, but he's not worth it twice. Nobody is. I wouldn't pay six million dollars for him if he were 12-feet tall. I'm sorry if that sounds heartless but I didn't get where I am by pouring my money down a toilet bowl. If we can get away with paying fifty, a hundred thousand, okay. But that's *it*."

"Spoken like a man suckled on the milk of human kindness," I said.

Vreel leaped out of his seat and threatened me with a sharp forefinger. "Look, hotshot, don't tell me you wouldn't do the same thing in my position. To tell you the truth, I'm still not entirely convinced this isn't some kind of publicity stunt engineered by you."

"Oh, Jesus, Mary and Joseph," I groaned.

"That's enough, you two!" the commissioner roared. He looked at me and sighed. "That was uncalled for, Dave."

I muttered an apology and the commissioner extracted one from Vreel. When breathing was down to normal, he resumed his lecture to the owner.

"You're still not thinking logically, Stanley. Again, we have to posit the worst, that because we refuse to pay the full ransom, these guys make good on their threat to kill Richie. What do you think will happen to us then? Even if we don't go to prison, do you think we'll ever have another moment's peace? Will anyone want to have anything to do with us again? Will we ever be able to look our friends and family in the eye? Will the press ever stop crucifying us down to our dying days? We'll be ruined men, Stanley. Is that worth saving three million dollars for? You tell me."

Vreel looked at the commissioner, then turned away and gazed at the wall with what, in combat, is known as the thousand-yard stare. For the first time, I felt a little sorry for the son of a bitch.

Now the commissioner looked at me. "You still want to go to the FBI, Dave?"

I gave a monumental shrug. "Commissioner, I don't think it makes any difference what I do. The chances of my getting out of this mess with my skin are slimmer than a flea's twat."

"Then that will be all for now, gentlemen," he said.

CHAPTER VII
• • • •

It had begun to rain, a fine misty drizzle that ventilated the city's canyons after a warm and humid day. I was caught without an umbrella but it was just as well. The cool moisture cleared my brain of the stagnation that had accumulated in the commissioner's office and damped down my furor with Stanley Vreel. I walked the two blocks to the St. Regis.

The Sadlers' suite was a chateau-sized complex high on the Fifth Avenue side. By craning your neck just a little you could see the immense green rectangle of Central Park stretching northward. With that for a backdrop, I faced Davis Sadler, his missus, and Sondra. Trish had spent the afternoon with them giving comfort and succor and she now faced me in the semicircle of brocaded chairs as if she were one of the family.

All four faces were drawn and fatigued and I was glad to have missed the first wave of emotion. Sondra seemed hardest hit of all, her puffy eyes and tangled hair indicating that that shell of blissful ignorance she'd surrounded herself with in Lauritzen's office had cracked as the realities finally broke through. Davis was grim but stolid, Bea a little out of it, I think because she'd drunk herself out of it. I couldn't blame her.

I told them the situation and briefed them on the conversation that had taken place in Commissioner Lauritzen's office. The mere fact that we had a plan, however tenuous, boosted everybody's spirits. Unlike myself, they had no misgivings about keeping the FBI out of the picture. They felt the FBI would only decrease the risk of getting Richie back safely. We probably have Watergate to thank for the Midwest's loss of faith in the official investigative branch of our government.

"What about this three million dollars?" Sadler asked. "Where is it going to come from?"

"The commissioner can swing a bank loan for part of it and put the arm on some owners for more."

"I think I could probably raise half a million," Sadler said.

"I'll tell that to the commissioner."

"How are we going to explain Richie's absence to the press?" he asked.

"We thought we'd say Richie is being kept in seclusion until his exams so that he bone up on schoolwork missed these last few weeks."

"Good, good. How about a drink, Bolt?"

"That would go down just fine, Mr. Sadler."

"Me too," Mrs. Sadler slurred.

"No, Bea, you've had enough." He looked at his daughter. "Sondra, help your mother to bed, she could use some sleep. And you might comb your hair and put on some make-up. You'll feel better."

With Trish's help, Sondra got poor old Bea to her feet and they staggered off to the bedroom. Sondra caught sight of herself in a mirror and blushed at her unkempt appearance. While they were out of the room, Sadler poured me a drink and said, "What do you think, Bolt?"

"Truthfully, sir? I think if it's a straightforward proposition of paying the ransom for Richie, the chances are good.

If we do anything else, our chances diminish."

"Of course, of course." Over this profound observation, we sat solemnly drinking until the women emerged. Sondra had restored her impeccable look and changed into a fresh, bright frock. I don't know what it did for her spirits but it did wonders for mine.

"I'm going to go down to the lobby and ask some questions," I said. "Maybe somebody down there remembers someone hanging around the lobby or something. Meanwhile, Mr. Sadler, Sondra, will you scour your memories and ask Mrs. Sadler to do the same when she's up to it? Try to remember if Richie got any strange phone calls or met anyone or took a girl out or went anywhere—you know the sort of thing I mean."

They looked at the ceiling, then at each other, then at me. They shook their heads.

"You can't think of anything, no matter how trivial, that might be a clue?"

At this point something curious occurred, something I did not pick up on at once because it didn't quite register at the time. What happened was that Sondra looked at her father as if expecting him to say something. His eyes darted sidelong, kind of defensively as if telling Sondra that whatever it was she wanted him to say, he wasn't about to mention it. Strange.

I sent Trish home but remained in the hotel and asked to see the manager, a Mr. Leescomb, a cordial gent with slicked-down hair. Apparently, no one had told him the wet-head look was dead. His smile was more professional than genuine and he got more proper with every question I asked until he dug his heels in, asked for my identification, and demanded to know what it was all about.

"Are you a detective?" he finally asked.

"Mr. Leescomb, do I talk like a detective?"

"No, but neither does Columbo."

"I'm Richie Sadler's agent," I said, flashing my card at him. As he examined it, I made up a good story. "He's been getting some crank calls and I'm trying to find out if there's any substance to them. Some of them threaten some rather dire things."

He relaxed a little. "Forgive me, Mr. Bolt. I get nervous when people begin asking questions. You remember what happened at the Pierre a few years ago."

I did. A gang of professional thieves took over the lobby in the small hours of the morning of January 2nd—when everyone was New Year's-weary—and methodically looted the safe-deposit boxes. There'd been some suspicion that it was an inside job, so naturally, Leescomb got uptight when people came snooping around.

He summoned the bell captain and a switchboard operator. The bell captain stood ramrod straight and could have been a bell regimental sergeant-major. I asked him if he remembered Richie coming or going with anyone besides his family or me but he could not, sir. Did he remember seeing anyone suspicious in the lobby? Thousands of strangers pass through the lobby daily, sir. Did he happen to notice any of them observing Richie? Many, sir—he attracts a great deal of attention. Anyone following him? Yes, sir: reporters autograph seekers, and pretty girls. Anyone asking for his room number? Yes, sir: reporters, autograph seekers, and pretty girls. Did he remember any of these pretty girls? All of them, sir, but none behaved in a manner one would describe as suspicious, just salacious.

I turned to the switchboard operator, a blue-haired old charmer who loved a mystery and answered my questions with relish. Did the hotel keep a record of incoming calls to guests? Oh no, that would be impossible. What about messages? Those were filed at the desk but once the guests picked them up that was the end of them. Did she remember anyone calling Richie Sadler? Oh my, he got lots of calls, particularly from tittering females but she had no way of knowing who the callers were. Did she ever happen to overhear...?

The woman scowled and her bosom swelled with indignation. "My dear young man..."

"Sorry! Sorry! Just trying to do my job, ma'am," I said in my best imitation of Jack Webb. "What about outgoing calls?

"Those we keep a record of, of course, for billing purposes. But if you're looking for telephone numbers, you won't find any on the local calls, just the long-distance ones."

"Can I see the bill anyway?"

She looked at Leescomb. Leescomb phoned upstairs and asked Davis Sadler for authorization to show me his bill. Sadler said, of course, and a few minutes later, a clerk arrived with the record of the Sadler party's telephone calls. I pounced on it and copied down the out-of-town numbers, almost all 312 prefixes, indicating Chicago area calls. I suspected these were calls to friends and relatives back home and to Sadler's office. This surmise proved correct on later investigation.

My last stab was at the message desk gal, a sweet young thing with big titties who batted her eyes at me but couldn't help me worth a damn as far as Richie was concerned. She didn't remember any of the names on the messages left for Richie, except that most of them ended in the letter "y"—Sandy, Barby, Suzy, Chrissy, Joany.

Leescomb pursed his lips. "I'm sorry, Mr. Bolt. It doesn't look as if you've learned anything very helpful."

I got to my feet wearily. "Oh, but I have. I've learned that I don't want to be a detective when I grow up... But you could do me a favor and speak to some of the other help, if you would—the bellboys, cleaning ladies, whoever."

"I will," Leescomb said, "and, oh yes, there are also the employees on other shifts. I'll be glad to speak to them when they come on duty."

"Good, good. You have my business card, Mr. Leescomb. If you hear of anything, you can call me at one of those numbers any hour of the day or night." I tapped my billfold ostentatiously. "Any information will be, um, amply acknowledged."

"We'll do all we can, Mr. Bolt," Leescomb said.

I imagine they did but I never heard from them again.

I went back to my apartment, a modest-sized two-bedroom flat in the Pavilion, a huge, block-square rabbit warren of an apartment complex on 77th Street and York Avenue. I was positively bushed and my thinking processes had ground to a halt. I hadn't eaten but wasn't especially hungry. I popped the top off a Falstaff, got into my jammies, and dozed off watching Johnny Carson.

I woke at 5 for my habitual nocturnal leak and struggled to sleep my way back into oblivion but was stampeded by bad fantasies: Richie had been snatched by the White Plains chapter of his fan club, by a band of short, jealous professional basketball players headed by Dean Meminger, Calvin Murphy, and Ernie Di Gregorio, by a sneaker manufacturer wanting him to do a free commercial, by Viktor Frankenstein, who wanted to give him a square haircut, affix bolts to his temples, and turn him loose on the countryside.

I wrestled with these images for an hour until I was damp with sweat and my bedclothes looked like a hooker's after a convention weekend. I got up and showered and made myself some bacon and eggs and my terrific eye-opening coffee whose formula will go with me to the grave. Over breakfast

I watched rosy-fingered dawn silhouette the Triboro Bridge until the sun rose brilliant and glary, promising a summery day. The coffee and sunlight cleared away the last creatures that had bedeviled my insomniac brain but left me with one marginally intriguing idea and one inspiration.

I decided to try these on the commissioner and phoned his home a little past 8. His wife told me he'd gone to the office early. I phoned there and he picked up the phone himself on the first ring. "Yes?" he said with tense expectancy.

"It's me, commissioner."

"Oh. Every time the phone rings..."

"I'm hip. Listen, I just wanted to give you an unprogress report and run a few ideas up the flagpole."

"Go ahead."

I told him about my inquiries at the hotel and read off the list of long-distance phone numbers dialed by the Sadlers from the St. Regis, asking him to have them checked out. Then I told him my marginally intriguing idea. "Do you think it could be the owner of another club? Don't laugh, now."

"I'm not laughing, Dave. I thought of it myself last night but rejected it. Look, owners are by definition greedy bastards but they're not kidnappers and murderers. An owner wants three million dollars, he raises his ticket prices a dollar and his hot dogs a dime and he's got his three million dollars."

"Maybe it wasn't done for the money."

"Then what for?"

"Some owner warned to clobber Vreel, hurt the league, force us to cancel the deal with Richie."

"It's possible but I still can't buy it. Businessmen don't operate that way."

"Even if they're associated with a certain underworld organization that rhymes with Shmoffa?"

"Especially then. You know something, Dave? The Mafia has a lower profile than Twiggy. The last thing the mob wants to do is something that will put it in the limelight. What do they need the heat for? When they can make three million dollars in one afternoon on the numbers or dope or loansharking, what's the percentage in committing a crime that'll have half the country eager to help the police solve it? Besides, there are no owners associated with the Mafia."

That was the league's official line and there was no point in calling him on it, though we both knew it to be patently untrue. But I did say, "I've heard some things about Hy Tishoff." This was understating the case by a power of 10.

"You think that because Tishoff lost out on Richie...? No, I can't believe it. Even if Tishoff was *Capo di Tutti Capi* for the North American continent, which is unlikely with a name like Tishoff... no Dave, you're definitely barking up the wrong tree. Nice try but no cigar. Any other ideas?"

"Yeah. Does the name Manny Ricci mean anything to you?"

"Sure. Gambler. And a loser."

"Do you remember his name coming up in connection with Richie's during the NCAA playoffs?"

"Of course. He's the one that accused Richie of double-crossing him in the Kentucky game, right? Silliest damn thing I've ever heard of."

"Agreed, but if you're looking for a motive..."

"Three million dollars is your motive, Dave. That's all you need."

"I suppose so."

"But you might try him. What the hell, it's better than sitting with our thumbs up our asses waiting for the phone to ring. Do you know where to reach him?"

"I was just going to ask you that."

"Call Lenny Weinstein. He's a living rogues' gallery of disagreeable human beings."

"Good idea."

"Stay in touch with me, Dave. I want to be ready to move when the kidnapper calls."

"You got it."

I got out my little black book and looked up Lenny Weinstein. Of the countless bookies I knew, he was one of the most knowledgeable and cooperative. And lest it seem odd that I know so many bookies, in my business they swarm thicker than flies around fresh dog shit. Throw your program up in the air at Madison Square Garden and the odds are 6-1 it'll land on a bookie's head. They're very helpful people to know, up to a point.

Lennie was an ugly, frenetic little sports nut who ran a semi-independent operation out of his apartment on Central Park West; he covered a lot of the action himself, but when the betting was heavy he laid off on organization bankrollers. I dialed his number with no expectation of reaching him and I didn't. I got a timid female voice with a thick Italian accent drowned out by the whine and thump of heavy machinery. "Shoe-a shop-a."

"I want Lenny Weinstein. Tell him it's Dave Bolt." I spelled it for her.

"You-a-number?"

I gave her my number and hung up. The shoe shop was Lennie's unofficial answering service.

I figured it would take a few minutes for Lenny to get back to me, so I called in to Trish. "What's in today's mail?"

"Dunning letters," she said, "but no good ones. Where are you?"

"Home and I may not be coming in till later. I'll call when I can, though, just in case. Keep the home fires burning and don't dip into the till."

"We have a till?" she said.

I hung up and was about to go into the kitchen for another cup of coffee when the phone rang. "Lightning?" It was Lenny, though he wouldn't identify himself.

"Yeah?"

"You called me?"

"Yeah."

"After all these years you're going to give me an inside tip?"

"Yeah," I said, "don't bet on the Pirate game today."

"Why not?"

"It's been called on account of rain."

"Fun-ny, fun-ny. What do you want?"

"A favor."

"Far vos? You never do anything for me."

"Next time you're indicted, I'll comfort your wife. Do you know Manny Ricci?"

"I don't associate with known underworld figures."

"Yeah, and I carry a spare dick in my hip pocket. I want to get hold of Ricci."

"How badly?"

"Serious badly."

"What's it worth to you?"

"I said it was a favor. A little turd like you never knows when he's gonna need a favor back. I have a long memory."

"Fuckin' guy," Weinstein complained to some phone-booth deity, "won't even tell me when one of his ballplayers sprains his little toe and I'm supposed to do him a favor. All right, I'll make some calls, I'll see. You wouldn't want to tell me what it's all about?"

"No."

"In case he asks?"

"I have a business proposition for him."

"Oh, for *him* you have a business proposition but for me you have diddlyshit."

"What can I tell you, Lenny? You're a diddlyshit kind of guy."

I made that second cup of coffee and decided to take care of a little agency business while waiting for word on—or from—Manny Ricci. I made several calls. To wit:

To Hal Flessas, a client of mine who'd rushed 1600 yards for New Orleans last year and wanted me to renegotiate his three-year contract—upwards, of course. Funny thing, but when they only rush five hundred they never ask me to renegotiate their contracts downward.

To Dave Curtis, the Nadler and Larimer ad agency executive handling the Brut Cologne account, to ask if Lonnie Seaforth could do that commercial for them. The answer was no, they were looking for superstars like Joe Namath and Hank Aaron, and Lonnie was only third-highest scorer in the NBA.

To Chickie Hanrahan, my pro golfer client, to tell him *Sports Illustrated* wanted to do an article on him. The crazy bastard wanted to turn it down unless they paid him to talk.

To Ferencz Borga, my Hungarian soccer player, to tell him the Pittsburgh Steelers would try him out as a place-kicker to back up the ailing Roy Gerela. Since I don't speak Hungarian and Borga's English is—to be kind—spotty, this conversation lasted 15 minutes and it nagged at me all day that he might have called the wrong ball club.

So it went, a typical morning in the life of a player's agent. I could have accomplished more, but I figured it was about time for Lenny Weinstein to call me, so I let the phone cool off. Ten minutes later, it rang.

"Bolt?"

It was a new voice to me, high and quivery, almost

squeaky. The guy spoke so close to the phone his "bs," "ps," and "ts" exploded like mortar shells and his "s's" hissed like steampipes. "Yes?"

"I unnerstan' you're tryin' to get a hold of Manny Ricci?"

"That's right. You him?"

"Maybe."

"Well, do you want to check it out and call me back?"

"Okay... What do you want, Bolt?"

"Do you know who I am?"

"The message said Dave Bolt."

"I mean, do you know . . . ?"

"Yeah, I know, I know. You're the agent. Whaddya want?"

"To talk."

"So? Talk."

"I mean, face to face."

There was a long pause filled with the stertorous rumble of his breath into the mouthpiece. Ricci was thinking it over and what he was thinking was, why should he see me? If he had Richie, he certainly had no interest in getting together with me. But even if he didn't, he still had good reason to be nervous. He was a man who lived in constant dread that he was going to be taken on a ride from which he would not return. For all he knew, I was setting him up to be hit.

"Look," I said soothingly, "you say when and where and how."

"You say why."

"Mutual interests."

"I didn't know we had any," he said.

"You don't call money interesting?"

"Depends. I call a lot of it interesting."

"Then tell me where I can see you. You call the shot."

He paused again and made a clicking sound with his tongue. "You know Queens?"

"Vaguely, yes."

"Awright, you go out to Queens Boulevard, to 67th Road. You coming by car?"

"I'll probably take the subway."

"Awright, you take the IND to 67th Street, you get out, you walk to 67th Road, that's one block. You cross Queens Boulevard and stand on the mall between the service road and the main drag facing *away* from the city. You got that so far?"

"Uh huh."

"You be there at 11 sharp and you stand there, I'll come around for you."

"How will you know it's me?"

"I'll know. You think *two* schmucks are gonna stand in the middle of Queens Boulevard for 15 minutes?"

He had a point there.

I repeated his instructions and looked at my watch. It was a little after 10. I left my apartment and walked over to the Lexington Avenue subway stop at 77th Street and took the IRT local to 51st Street. There was no transfer to the IND at the stop, so I had to go outside to Lexington, walk up to 53rd, and catch the Queens train at the IND station there. The trip was noisy and even if there'd been anything to see, I would not have been able to make it out through the blue paint of an immense graffito sprayed on the window.

I flinched from the strong sunlight as I trudged up the stairs of the 67th Street station and out onto Queens Boulevard, a broad avenue and one of the main thoroughfares between Manhattan and Long Island. It had two express roads three lanes wide each, flanked by two-lane service roads separated from the express roads by concrete malls covered with subway gratings. I was standing in front of a supermarket. In one direction was a fast-food phenomenon called the Knish Knosh and in the opposite direction, toward Manhattan, some shops, a bank, and a movie theater called the Trylon. Everything else was red brick apartment houses. It was not a very glamorous community but it was the perfect environment for a punk gambler—Deep Jimmy Breslin Country, I would call it. I panned the scene hoping to get a glimpse of Ricci but aside from an old man double-parked waiting for his wife to come out of a bakery, I saw no one. But I knew I was being watched.

I walked to 67th Road and bought a knish at the Knish Knosh. It was better than some I've eaten, but as far as I'm concerned, all knishes have the consistency of black-eyed peas wrapped in lizard skin. This Jewish chick I went with for a few months, Eileen Gordon, tried to turn me on to Jewish cooking but aside from Eileen herself I found most of it inedible. When you've been raised on Meskin chili and jalapeños, pot roast and potato pancakes are apt to leave you a little flat.

Munching on my knish, I crossed the service road at the corner of Queens Boulevard and 67th Road and stood on the mall, looking around and feeling vulnerable and stupid under the curious glances of car passengers. Ten minutes went by and I began to get a little dizzy from inhaling carbon monoxide. To entertain myself, I played license-plate poker with myself and had just drawn a Queens-up full house on a New Jersey plate when a horn honked behind me. I turned and saw a man in a blue polo shirt and baseball cap waving at me from the driver's seat of a late model green Buick that was holding up traffic in the westbound express lane. I darted through a cluster of eastbound cars, crossed in front of the Buick, and hopped into the passenger seat. I found myself looking at a little man holding a big gun. "Put your hands on the dashboard, Bolt," he said to me in a tenor voice.

"Sure, friend, it's your game all the way." I learned in the Army when a .45 automatic addresses you, you listen very, very respectfully.

We bucked forward and cut toward the inside of the boulevard. Ricci drove with his left hand, covered me with his right while looking anxiously into his rearview mirror; I hoped he had better coordination than he had indicated so far. At the first exit, he swerved into the westbound service road, made a sharp right through a red light at the Rego Park intersection where Alexander's Department Store is, then snaked around the streets of Lefrak City until I lost track of his weaving maneuvers. I closed my eyes and tried to relax but I felt this itch in my midsection where the automatic's slug would enter making a large neat hole and emerge making a huge ragged one.

When we finally stopped, I opened my eyes and saw that we were on a quiet residential street a convenient few hundred yards from an entry ramp to the Van Wyck Expressway, a perfect escape route if he sensed this was some sort of trap. He kept the motor idling. He was a very nervous man.

I looked at him. He reminded me of a ferret, with a long, lumpy gullet and tiny ears sticking out beneath his Mets baseball cap. He looked more like a Walt Disney character than a gangster but the siege weapon he trained on my vital organs kept my laughter down to a minimum.

"Now, you wanted to talk to me," he said.

"Yes."

"About?"

"About a funny thing that happened to one of my clients the other day."

"What's that?"

I looked at him squarely. His eyes were dark and red-rimmed and they constantly darted to his rearview mirror.

They told me nothing except that he was as jumpy as a gentile in the Catskills.

"Someone borrowed him and won't give him back," I said.

I scrutinized his face for a reaction and I hoped for a guilty one. There was none, guilty or otherwise.

"He's being held for ransom?" Ricci said.

"Uh huh."

"Is this a ballplayer, a star or something?"

"Uh huh."

He nodded appreciatively. "It's a good gimmick. I've thought of doing it myself."

"How recently?"

Holding the gun on me with his right hand, he reached up with his left and pulled a Camel out of a pack attached to his car visor with a rubber band, pushed in his cigarette lighter, and lit up with a smacking sound.

"So? Who put the snatch on your boy?"

"Can't you guess?"

"How the fuck should I know? I don't know who you represent." He dragged hard on the cigarette while his eyes roved the roof of the car reflectively. "But then, I'm asking myself why you came to *me.*"

"Good thinking."

"I do know the name of one of your guys."

"I know you do."

He looked at me searchingly and this time it was my turn to say nothing with my eyes. "If it's who I'm thinkin'..." He broke into a horrible stained-toothed grin. "I hope they take a baseball bat to his kneecaps before they dump that cocksucker back on your doorstep."

"Nice talk," I said. "What did he ever do to you?"

"You know fuckin' well what he did to me. That's why you're here, ain't it? You think I snatched Richie Sadler.

Well, I'll tell you something. I wish I had. I wouldn't ask for a cent in ransom. Just the chance to teach him the proper way to shave points. I'd shave the point off his—"

"Say, Manny?" I interrupted him as pleasantly as I knew how. "Did you know, your trigger finger goes in and out when you're mad? What worries me is, it's gonna go in a little too far and you're gonna shoot me before we can finish our conversation. So what I'm getting around to is, maybe you ought to put the gun down, what do you say?"

He studied me. I had my honest dumb cowboy face going for me. He grunted and lowered the gun to his lap.

"Thank you," I said. "Now, what about this point shaving bit?"

"'Bit?'"

"Well, what do you call it, Manny?"

"I call it the biggest double-cross since Hitler invaded Russia."

"Can you elaborate on that?"

"You read about it. The spread is 15. That's a gambler's dream. I take Kentucky, if it's a fairly close game I win, right? So I call Richie..."

"Wait a minute, wait a minute. How do you know Richie?"

"I met him at a chamber music concert."

"Come on, Manny, this is serious business."

"Let's just say I was innerduced to him. I cultivate athletes. That's how I get my edge. That's how any gambler gets his edge."

"He knew you were a gambler?"

"Sure," he grinned.

"Manny," I said, "why are you sticking to this preposterous story? Do you think I'm trying to trick you into telling me the real one so I can go tell your mob or something? I mean, I don't understand you."

"I don't give a fuck who you don't understand, mister, I'm telling you what happened."

"The gun again, Manny."

He had unconsciously raised it and waving it around for emphasis. To my relief, he set it down again in his lap.

"I'm telling you, I call Richie and I says to him, 'Let's get together.' So we get together and I tell him I have a proposition that could make him twenty-five large ones. All he has to do is hold the score under 15. He says, 'For fifty you got it.' So I call my people and they bet everything but their first-born on Kentucky. And that cocksucker scores 48 points."

I had to laugh, it was so incredible. "Manny, leaving aside for the moment the fact that your story makes Watergate look like the gospel truth, why would Richie double-cross you?"

"Because someone paid him more money. A *lot* more money."

"You mean another syndicate or something?"

"That's right."

"And who might that be?"

"Provenzano. He personally won two million on that game, I happen to know—and I can tell you he don't bet a quarter on anything that ain't rigged ten ways from the middle."

"And you think some of that went to Richie?"

"Damn right. How else you gonna explain it?"

"How about this one, that you're a big fuckup? That you've invented this... this story to take the heat off you with your people?"

Ricci gave me a pathetic look. "Christ, won't nobody listen to me!" He pounded the steering wheel with his fist. "Anyway," he sighed, "I don't have Richie Sadler."

"I'd already figured that out. Do you have any idea who does?"

"I ain't heard nothin', not word one."

"There's a healthy reward for you if you should find out anything about his whereabouts.

"He looked at me sadly. "You could offer me Chase Manhattan, I wouldn't know where to begin. But I'll tell you one thing, it ain't the mob. The mob don't operate that way."

"So everybody keeps telling me."

"I'll drive you back if you want."

"I'd be obliged.

He threaded the Buick back to Queens Boulevard and pulled up in front of the Continental Avenue station, an express stop. As I reached for the door handle, he said, "Just out of curiosity, how much are they asking for Richie?"

"A hell of a lot of loot."

"You gonna pay it?"

I believed that the question was asked out of simple curiosity but I decided not to give him an honest answer anyway. To tell him yes was to invite an epidemic of kidnappings.

"We're disinclined."

"Good. I hope they bury him alive and pull out the air hose."

"You sure are good folks," I said, opening the door and stepping out. Then I remembered something. "I don't suppose you can keep our little meeting quiet?"

He looked at me with dead eyes. "Mister, you don't seem to understand, I got nobody to tell."

CHAPTER VIII

• • • •

I got back to the office around 3 to find Trish in a rampaging tizzy. Her desk was a litter of undecipherable messages, unfiled folders, unopened mail, an uneaten sandwich, and an untouched cup of coffee. Her hair was uncombed, her clothes unkempt, and her temper unkept. She held the phone under her chin and was burrowing through the mess looking for a pen and something to write on. "Okay, got it!" she shouted, writing a message down on a paper napkin and slamming the phone down. The ink blotted into an oval blob.

She looked up and saw me. "Jesus, what a day you picked not to come to the office!"

"Anybody call?"

"Anybody? Everybody! The Pope, the Queen, Lee Duc Tho, the Messiah, they all called. I haven't had a bite to eat and I couldn't get to the post office and if I don't pee *this second* there's gonna be an accident."

I brushed a wisp of hair out of her eyes. "All right, all right, calm down. Just tell me, did Vreel or the commissioner call?"

"No. They're the only ones who didn't call."

"Okay, go pee."

"It may be too late," she said, scattering paper until she found the powder-room key.

She dashed out and I shuffled the papers around, separating telephone memo slips from the rest and examining them as they surfaced. There were a lot of them, mostly urgent ones from clients. I set them aside. They could wait. When a client calls you urgently, it means he needs an advance.

Three messages aroused my curiosity, all from non-clients. One was from Sondra Sadler, another from my best friend Roy Lescade, the *New York Post* sportswriter, and third was from my pal up in Harlem, Tatum Farmer. All were marked *Urgent,* and the one from Lescade said, typically, "Call me back or you die!"

I loved Roy better than a brother. He was a good old boy from Brownsville, Tex. He'd played for Texas A&M, linebacker and every year for three years, whenever the Aggies played the Longhorns we'd beat each other's asses off. He was drafted by the Chicago Bears but was essentially lazy and failed to make the cut. His daddy wanted him to run the ranch but Roy loved sports too much—and besides, he'd discovered a hidden talent for writing. So he set out to be a sports reporter. He'd become one of the best, for my money, and one of the few I liked to read because he was honest. He boasts he makes up only 10 percent of what he writes which is an incredible display of integrity.

He also cares, not just about sports and athletes but about people. He's always going after the human-interest side of a story and it was one such story, about a former Dallas Cowboy who'd dropped out of football after an injury and almost destroyed himself with drink, that led to the rescue of the author of this account. It was Roy who got me a job in the front office of the Cowboys and Roy who suggested I had a good feel for the agency business. Shit, it was even Roy who suggested I ought to write down some of the things that have happened to me and try to get them published. So you can see how much I owe Roy Lescade.

I called him first and slipped easily into my cowboy bag.

"You leave this message for me, you old turd?"

"Dave! Hiya, buddy!"

"What's up?"

"I wanted to tell you the one about the Polack who's making love to his girlfriend?"

"The Polack who's making love to his girlfriend," I repeated, searching my mind. "No, I don't think I heard that one."

"Well," Roy said, chuckling, "she says to him, 'Kiss me where it smells.' "

"Yeah?"

"So he drove her to Gary, Ind." He broke into an explosive hissing giggle.

"Good one, Roy. What'd you call about?"

"Oh, I thought you might help me puzzle out a weird thing that's going on. You know I been taking out Commissioner Lauritzen's secretary, Connie?" Roy ended most sentences with a question mark.

"Sure I know. You took her away from me, remember, buddy-fucker?"

"Bullshit! You said you were through with her. Anyway, I was talking to her last night—uh, to tell the truth, I was bailing her ass off—and she told me there was some big kind of hassle concerning Richie?"

"No trouble, Roy," I extemporized, silently cursing both of them. "A hitch came up, that's all. We were dickering over some small print and the parties got a little sore at each other, it don't amount to nothing more'n that." I waited to see if Roy would buy it. If I knew him, he wouldn't.

"Didn't sound that way to me but Connie refused to tell me anything more. I called Richie at his hotel? Got his sister, the one you were talking to at the party? Pretty little thing, she is."

"What'd she say?"

"She said he's 'in seclusion.' Dave, what the fuck is that supposed to mean?"

"He's got to bone up for his final exams, that's all. Too many damn reporters hounding him, if you get what I mean."

"That's what she said, he's studying. And what Vreel said, too."

"You've spoken to Vreel?"

"Uh huh."

"Busy little reporter, ain't you?"

"Got to earn those Yankee dollars, buddy. I also had an interesting conversation with Tommy Brent?"

"Tommy Brent?" I frowned. Tommy was the owner of the St. Louis Gateways of the ABA.

"Yeah, he was bitching about being hit up for an extra assessment for Richie Sadler?"

"But Roy, all the owners..."

"This is a *second* assessment. Now, can I come over?"

"I don't really have the time, Roy. Ever since Richie Sadler I been busier'n a sow with four tits and eight piglets."

"That's what I call a buddy." He sighed. "All right, I guess I'll just have to print my speculations."

"What kind of speculations?"

"Oh, that the deal is about to fall through, maybe?"

That was what I'd hoped Roy would say, not because I wanted that printed but because it indicated he was still in the dark as to what the problem was with Richie. The best thing to do was to string him along.

"You sure are one smart sumbitch," I said, trying to sound a little awestruck.

"Aw shit, Dave, it's just that I've seen so many contracts tore up in my time, I can hear one ripping five miles away."

I played him like a hooked fish. "Tell you what, Roy, you git your syph-ridden ass up here in half an hour, I'll give you the poop—on the condition you don't release it till I say go. Fair?"

"Fair."

"And don't breathe a word to nobody, hear?"

"Shucks and I was just about to call Dick Young at the *News.*"

My next call was to the St. Regis Hotel. I asked for the Sadler suite and got Sondra.

"Any news?" she asked. She sounded terribly tired and strained.

"Not yet."

"Nothing yet," she repeated to her parents.

"What about you?" I asked. "You called, said it was urgent."

She hung fire so long I thought we'd been cut off. "Well, yes."

Something suddenly occurred to me. "Are you free to talk, Sondra?"

"Not really," she said in a level voice.

"Are you all right?"

"Oh sure," she singsonged.

"Are you free to come and go?" My heart was pumping hard. I wondered if someone was holding a gun to her head.

"Of course."

"All right. Meet me at my apartment at 7. We'll have dinner and talk." I gave her the address.

"That'll be fine."

I hung up and scratched my head. Someone in the room

with Sondra had inhibited her from speaking freely, yet she was free to come and go and didn't seem overly uptight. Maybe she wanted to tell me something she didn't want her parents to hear. I hearkened back to what had happened yesterday when I'd asked them if they could think of anything else that might be helpful. Sondra and her father had exchanged a funny look. I hadn't thought anything of it then but now I wondered if there was some skeleton in the family closet that was rattling the doorknob. I speculated on what it might be but found my speculations drifting to another possible outcome of dinner with Sondra at my apartment. Had Trish not returned, grinning the grin of one who has found a blissful relief, it's hard to say where my fantasies would have carried me.

Trish began cleaning up her desk but I didn't want her around when Roy came by. Roy could charm the birds out of the trees. He'd already jollied enough out of Connie, Commissioner Lauritzen's gal Friday, to jeopardize the secrecy of our situation. I felt Trish was made of sterner stuff than Connie but I wasn't about to put this hypothesis to the test. I pressed two dollars into her hand for a taxi and sent her home. She looked at the deuce and said, "Wow, boss. Ever since you took on Richie Sadler the money has been flowing like—silk."

"If you think that's small, wait till you see your severance pay," I said holding the door open for her.

While I waited for Roy, I called Tatum Farmer. Tatum called me regularly with tips about interesting ballplayers coming up in Harlem but this was the first time he'd said it was something urgent. I thought maybe he simply had an *urgently* interesting ballplayer coming up, but as soon as I heard his voice I knew something was seriously wrong.

"Dave? Aw, thanks for calling me back, Dave," he said as if I'd just rescued him from the gallows. His voice was nasal and mournful and seemed to be fogged from crying.

"Jesus, what is it, Tatum?"

"Oh it's bad, Dave. Bad, bad, bad."

"Tell me, for Christ's sake."

"Timmie Lee, the kid we played with the other day?"

"Yeah?"

"They got him, Dave. They beat him up somethin' terrible." He started snuffling and I waited nervously. "They broke him up so bad he'll never play basketball again. Fuck, the hospital says he may never even regain consciousness."

"Who did it, Tatum? Who's 'They'?"

"I don't know for sure but I can guess."

"Slakey?"

"That's who *I* think."

I lowered myself into my chair. "Tell me just what happened."

I drummed the desk while he blew his nose and lit a cigarette. "You saw him that day, how he had his arm around Timmie and all that shit?"

"Yes."

"Well, he been sweet-talkin' Timmie the last couple of weeks, I mean, rushin' him hard, you understand? Tryin' to get him to sign an agreement, like an exclusive contract?"

"Why, those are worthless, Tatum. For one thing, the kid's only a minor."

"The kid don't know that and Slakey wouldn't care anyway. Once he's got a kid signed up, he's got him locked."

"Is that what happened?"

"Yes. Last week Timmie told me he was gonna 'sign up' with Slakey as soon as he could come up with the 'consideration' of five hundred bucks Slakey required. I think Timmie was thinking of hitting *me* up for that five but I set him straight fast enough. I tried to talk him out of it. I tried to make him go see you and talk it over with you, but you know, some of these kids don't trust The Man, you understand. Well, two days later he calls me and says, 'Hey, Tatum, do you think Slakey's jivin' me?' I says, 'What do you mean, boy?' He says, 'Well, I come up with five bills Tuesday and today Slakey calls me and says I owe him another two hundred and fifty.' I says, 'What for?' He says, 'On account of Slakey says he talked to John Wooden of UCLA.' "

I rubbed the bridge of my nose. "What does one thing have to do with another?"

"Don't you see?" Tatum said, sniffing. "John Wooden is the most famous coach in the country. Even the dumbest kid in Harlem knows who he is. What Slakey was saying was, for getting through to Wooden, he deserved kind of like a bonus."

"What did you tell Timmie?"

"I told Timmie, 'Boy, you been fucked over for fair. Get out of this before he owns you.' And you know what Timmie says? Timmie says, 'I think you may be right, Tatum.' And that's the last thing he said to me."

"Last night, he told his mother he was gonna have a talk with Slakey. He never come back. This morning some kids found him on some rubble in a lot on 133rd Street. They'd taken a pipe to his arms and legs and for good measure stomped on his head. Aw, Dave, he was a good boy..."

Tatum's voice cracked again and he began sobbing. I felt sympathetic tears filling my eyes and I sat quietly in my darkening office waiting for Tatum to get control. Finally, he said, "Dave?" His voice had an ominous quality.

"Yes?"

"I'm going after him."

"You're gonna do no such thing, Tatum."

"I'm gonna kill that motherfucker." He was frighteningly calm and I knew he meant it.

"Listen to me, Tatum. You take this upon yourself, many things can happen, all of them bad."

"What am I supposed to do, stand by and watch him rip these kids off and beat them into vegetables? There's a beautiful boy layin' in Harlem Hospital tonight who ain't gonna be good for playin' jacks let alone basketball, if he comes out at all. Ain't no *way* I'm gonna sit for that!"

"There's a better way."

"Don't hit me with any 'Work Within The System' jive. That may work downtown but up here it don't buy a thimbleful of shit. They sent a couple of detectives around. The detectives said, 'The kid must have been dealing dope,' and went back to the precinct. I'm telling you true, Dave, I'm gonna go after that motherfucker and I'm gonna lace his face with my kitchen knife."

"Come on, Tatum. I know you know the difference between right and wrong and what you're talking about is wrong, uptown or down. I know what kind of pain you're in but you take action blindly and you're gonna end up in a gutter or a prison cell or a wooden box and you won't have made the world a better place by the thickness of one hair."

Tatum breathed heavily into the phone for a minute, negotiating in his grief-stricken mind between vengeance and common sense. Finally, he said, "You got a better plan?"

"I think I can come up with one."

"Like what?"

At that moment the door opened and the hulking, rain coated figure of Roy Lescade tramped in. "I got someone in my office now, Tatum. Give me till tomorrow. I want to speak to some people. Will you do that?"

"Till tomorrow, all right. But you better come up with something good, because I'm gonna take that motherfucker *off.*"

I hung up and swung around in my chair. Roy was

standing in the anteroom poking his head into my darkened office like a suspicious bear. His was a massive presence that threw a huge shadow across the carpet. Roy was an inch shorter than me but he had the shoulders and chest of a buffalo. Had he wanted to work at it, Roy could have been one of the greatest defensive football players of all time; I think he could have been an even better linebacker than Dick Butkus. But he just didn't have that desire.

"That you, lardass?" I said.

"What you doin' in the dark, Dave?"

"Playin' with myself."

He ambled in and walked straight to my liquor cabinet. "Seems kind of silly considering that piece of poon you keep for a secretary. Where is she? I'm workin' on that, you know."

"I know. I lock her up when you come over."

He helped himself to a bourbon and reached behind a bookshelf where he knew I kept my branch water, something I save for drinkers with civilized palates. He made me one without asking if I wanted it and we quaffed in silence for a couple of minutes before getting down to serious conversation.

"Now then, Thunder Bolt, what is going on with Richie Sadler?"

"Well," I said, digging in for a good bluff, "like you guessed, the negotiations came apart at the last minute. Not fatally, you understand. Let's just say the contracts are on the runway but I can't quite get 'em into the sky."

"What's the problem?"

"Richie is asking for a loan."

"A loan? How much?"

"Yea much."

He polished off his drink and lumbered to the cabinet for a refill. "Must be an awful lot, Dave. He's got people running around like wild ponies trapped in a box canyon."

"Seven digits, not counting the two on the other side of the decimal point."

"What for?"

"He wants to build a sporting-goods store," I said, congratulating myself on my inventiveness. "You know, something he can count on for income when he retires."

"Retires! He ain't even started yet!"

"Oh, you know how these kids think nowadays."

He shook his head and nattered like a horse. "Sporting-goods store."

"That's right."

"Where is he?"

"I told you, in seclusion, and that's the truth. He's got to hit the books for exams or he won't get his diploma and won't that be embarrassing?"

"Can't I at least...?"

"Interview him? No. But as soon as this thing gets cleared up, I'll give you the exclusive, I give you my word as a white man." I raised my hand in a solemn vow.

He looked unhappy but accepting. Then he suddenly cried, "Hey, you *ain't* a white man, you sumbitch!" He threw an ice cube at me. "You're part black!"

"And you better remember it, honky."

We refilled, or more properly re-refilled, clowned a little, and reminisced about growing up in Texas. Roy spun a long and probably apocryphal yarn about his first sex experience, with Paloma, his Mexican nanny. "She was a handsome widow that was always being eyed by the hands," Roy said, "and they would have caught her too, except my daddy had warned them he'd cut the pecker off the first man that touched her. Actually, daddy was saving her for himself. Anyway, one day, we were walking near the corral, Paloma and me, when I saw something I'd never seen before. My daddy was feeding the cock of this inexperienced stallion into a mare's pussy. I'd seen plenty of animals mating, you understand, but this was new to me. Well, I felt myself getting hard and Paloma noticed the bulge in my trousers.

"Suddenly my daddy spied us and chased us away; he thought I was too young to be witnessing this business. So Paloma and I went back to the ranch house. Ain't nobody there. Paloma says, 'You want play horse?' I says sure. So she undoes my pants and takes out my whang and lifts her skirts and does like my father did with the stallion. Then she showed me another way, and a couple of others. That gal had one big repertory; I'll tell you. We played horse every chance we got until daddy, on account of Paloma was indifferent to his advances, got suspicious that some hand was banging her regular. One day I was riding high on Paloma when guess who busts into my room? Well, he gives me a whipping so bad I still got stripes on my ass. And Paloma? He drug her out to the corral, screaming, 'You like to play horse, I'll give you a *real* stallion to hump!' It was too dark for me to see proper, but the sound of her screams—I still dream about them. Never saw her after that."

I listened to Roy's tale with attention divided by concern. Richie was uppermost but the sound of Tatum's sobs still echoed in my head. In a way, the problem of heading off Tatum was even more pressing than Richie, because if I didn't do something about it tonight, he was going to do something about Slakey tomorrow. I had to stop him.

Suddenly I looked at Roy and realized he might hold the answer. "Hey Roy, how would you like to cover a *real* story?"

He tilted his head. "You don't call Richie Sadler's contract a real story?"

"Hell," I sneered, "Anybody can write that big headline shit. I'm talking about a human-interest story, the kind you do so well."

He looked askance at me. "You wouldn't be trying to divert my attention from the Sadler story, would you?"

"With all we been through together, you still distrust me?" I said indignantly.

"With all we been through together, you should thank your stars I'm talking to you at all. What's this human-interest story?"

I began relating the story of Timmie Lee and Warnell Slakey and the deeper I went into it, the more attentive and sober he became. When I came to the beating, he held his breath and leaned forward with his elbows on his knees. His eyes took on a distant cast as if he were framing the story in some larger context in his mind. When I finished, he swallowed hard.

"Well?" I said. "What do you think?"

He sighed. "I got to admit, it's a heckuva story, Dave." He asked me a few questions, then reflected quietly. "Funny thing but in my mind there's some sort of link-up between the Timmie Lee story and Richie Sadler's, as if... as if Timmie's is the other side of the coin. The coin..." He closed his eyes and visualized it. "The coin is ambition and greed and folly. It's the common currency of the privileged white kid from Midwest suburbia and the disadvantaged black from the deep ghetto of Harlem. Here's a white kid with a three million-dollar contract that ain't good enough for him. And here's a black kid who'd be happy to have 1 percent of that and will go to any lengths to get it. Ambition and greed and folly. Christ!"

I looked away from Roy, ashamed of myself for having misled him about Richie, yet strangely touched anyway, as if Roy's interpretation, with only a few adjustments, might be true. Because for every Richie who accepted life's bounty with humility and gratitude, there were a dozen vain, arrogant athletes who believed nobody could ever pay them what they were worth. I knew, I represented some of them.

"How would you like to help me put Warnell Slakey out of business?" I said to Roy.

"Nothing would give me greater pleasure."

"Okay. Call me tomorrow. I'll have my strategy thunk about by then."

"I'd like to visit Timmie Lee tonight."

"You got it." I phoned Tatum Farmer and let Roy speak to him. They arranged to meet at Harlem Hospital.

Roy left quickly, leaving me sitting in the shadows, depressed about the human condition and filled with a longing for sleep or some other kind of oblivion that would remove me from the vileness I'd seen the last few days. I looked at the bottle of bourbon on the liquor cabinet. There was more than enough to narcotize myself for 10 or 12 hours. It was my first strong temptation in a decade. Then I remembered I had a date with Sondra Sadler at 7. I looked at my watch. It was 7.

The mere thought of her, oddly, chased the bogeys out of my brain. I put the bourbon back in the liquor cabinet, locked up the office, and hurried out of the darkened building.

I hailed a cab. It was still light out and the evening was still warm. We headed up Third Avenue. It was swarming with carefree couples reveling in the simple splendor of a perfect spring evening in New York. My driver, a long-haired kid, stopped for a light and we watched a thousand pleasure-seekers bustle past us heading for Bloomingdale's and Alexander's and Yellowfingers and Daly's and the movie theaters that line Third Avenue between 57th and

60th Streets. The cabby looked over his shoulder at me and said, "You know what?"

"What?"

"Life can be real nice."

"Gee, I'd have expected something more profound from a guy like you."

"There's nothing profounder," he said.

I thought of Sondra and my pulse quickened. "Maybe you're right about that."

CHAPTER IX

• • • •

As we swung into the pretentious blue-fountained portico of the Pavilion, I saw Sondra pacing the cavernous lobby looking in bewilderment at her wristwatch. It was almost 7:30. She looked very fetching in a clingy jersey dress, an interesting departure, I reflected, from her customary modest and unrevealing attire.

I thanked the driver and gave him a 15-cent override on my traditional quarter tip for his reaffirmation of life and hopped out. The uniformed doorman gave the revolving door a push for me and I took Sondra's arm.

"Sorry I'm late. It's been one of those days."

"Any news?"

"No. A few possibilities eliminated but I'm afraid nothing on the positive side."

She nodded in a kind of mute resignation and we got on the elevator. The ride up was awkward and we kept our eyes forward as if to reassure each other that this was not a social engagement. It was unthinkable to me that our concern for Richie could be tainted by thoughts of a romantic nature. So why did I have these thoughts of a romantic nature?

"I'm afraid I'm not prepared for guests," I said unlocking my door. "Place is kind of a mess and I don't have any meat defrosted."

"Oh, we can rustle something up."

"I'm good on short-order stuff," I said eagerly.

"You're a man of many parts."

"Shoot, a plateful of bacon and eggs doesn't make someone a man of many parts." I pushed the door open. "Well," I said with a sweep of the hand, "there it is. The rent was ridiculous when I moved in four years ago and they've raised it twice since then, to Fantastic and then to Drop Dead. But at least it's hot in the summer and cold in the winter and you can't punch a hole in the wall unless you're real mad."

She looked around appraisingly, made some obligatory "oohs" and "ahhs" about my view of the Triboro Bridge, which at that moment was picking up the last glint of the setting sun, then turned to my lithographs. She studied them with a professional, hands-behind-the-back posture. "These are quite nice," she said. There was a note of surprise in her voice.

"Oh, just something an artist friend gave me."

"Who is he?"

"She," I corrected her, feeling an unaccountable flush of embarrassment suffusing my cheeks.

"Ah."

"Will you have something to drink?"

"Maybe some white wine on the rocks."

"You got it."

I uncorked a bottle of Chablis and poured out two glasses. I opened a jar of smoked walnuts and dropped into my pony-upholstered sling chair opposite the suede sofa where Sondra sat with her feet curled beneath her. I raised my glass "To Richie's safe return."

"Yes."

I sipped my wine. "You sounded pretty uptight on the phone."

"I couldn't talk."

"Because of your father?"

She raised one eyebrow. "Why, yes. How did you know?"

"What was so secret you couldn't discuss it in front of him?"

She compressed her lips. "Just something I've been thinking. My father... well, you see... um, when I think about it, it seems so . . . why don't we forget about it?"

She sipped at her wine and shook her head in disgust.

"Look," I said, "maybe it's silly but maybe it's not. Why don't you tell me? I promise not to have you executed.''

She swished her wine around for a minute, then sighed. "It's something—a remark my father made last year when everybody was talking to us about the fantastic salaries ballplayers make, you know?"

"Yes?"

"Well, we were sitting around the dinner table and daddy said—it was only a joke, you understand—he said, 'You know, with all these valuable ballplayers around, it's a wonder nobody's ever kidnapped one and held him for ransom.'"

My mouth dropped open. "Your father said that?"

"Yes, but *jokingly.* You have to understand, he's always saying things like that."

"But in this context..." I said, wondering. "He didn't want you to tell me this, did he?"

"No, because he knew it would sound suspicious in view of what's happened."

"That's for sure. And yet—well, why would a man have his own son kidnapped? For money, maybe, except your dad is well fixed. Hell, he even said he could raise half a million himself, toward the ransom. No, I think it's just what it appears to be—an innocent remark that turned out to be a dead-on prediction."

"Yes, she said, "except..." She picked at a piece of rug lint on my sofa. There was something more.

"Except what, Sondra?"

"Except that his behavior... he's been doing an odd thing since we came to New York."

"How do you mean?"

"Well, he goes out in the afternoon or evening for hours at a time and nobody knows where."

"Have you asked him?"

"Yes. He says he's been seeing business associates but he gets very evasive when mother or I try to pin him down. And two days ago, the day before Richie disappeared? Daddy went out in the afternoon and when he came back he said he'd been having drinks with this old friend of his, Paul Gaines of Mutual of New York. Well, mother called Paul and Paul didn't even know we were still in town!"

"Where do you think he goes?" I asked.

"Well, Paul jokingly implied that daddy must have a..." She made a face.

"A lady friend?"

"Yes."

"What do you think?"

"He's never struck me as... that kind. And mother says, to her knowledge daddy's never... daddy's always been true."

"Tell me about the relationship between Richie and your father."

She shrugged and stared. "Isn't it obvious? They're like this." She held up two intertwined fingers. "Of course, it wasn't always that way. In fact, they used to fight a great deal."

"About what?"

"About a lot of things but somehow they always boiled

down to basketball. See, daddy had this idea that Richie could be the greatest—I mean, *the* greatest. But Richie had other interests besides basketball. For a while, he was interested in becoming an actor. Then he talked about traveling. But whatever he wanted, daddy would say no, you've got to be a basketball player.

"It all came to a head over this girl Richie started seeing, Shawna Parks. Richie was really in love with her and talked about marrying her in his junior year and then going into daddy's insurance business when they graduated. Well, daddy made his life so miserable they finally broke up. Richie was heartbroken for about six months. Then daddy took him fishing and they talked and Richie realized daddy was right, that with hard work he really could become *the* greatest basketball player of all time. Since then, they've been—well, as I said, great pals."

"What does your mother do every day?"

"She goes out shopping. And she really does. She comes back with something every day. It's almost a compulsion with her."

"Yes, but that she comes back with something every day doesn't necessarily mean..."

"My mother?" Sondra laughed. "Forget it. My mother is dingbat city, she hasn't got a larcenous cell in her body."

"And you're pretty certain you're reading your parents right?"

She laughed nervously. "Gee, I *think* so. I mean, I don't think I have too many hang-ups about them."

"No, your hang-up is about Richie."

She frowned. "What's that supposed to mean?"

"Just that—well, you're pretty crazy about him."

"Shouldn't I be?" Her voice quavered defensively warning me I was probing what this psychiatrist friend of mine calls sensitive material.

"Sure, but I suspect you deny yourself a lot of things on account of him."

"Yes, I guess I do. In many ways he's the most important man in my life." She fixed me with an intense emerald gaze. "You think he's keeping me from getting involved with other men?"

"You do sink an awful lot of energy into that boy. Do you, uh, go out much?"

"Of course, I go out. It's just that there's never been anybody..."

"As good as your brother." As soon as I said it I could have bitten my tongue. She withered me with a flamethrower look and fingered her purse as if thinking of leaving.

"You sound almost jealous," she said.

"Me? Jealous?" I laughed. "What have I got to be jealous of?" But even as I said it I knew she was right.

She suddenly looked confused and embarrassed. "I'm sorry. That was very presumptuous of me, wasn't it?"

"No, not if the presumption is that I like you."

I was glad I said it, but the interplay now collapsed in a fluster and we both sat sipping our wine for a minute in anguished silence.

Finally, she said, "Is that your wife and daughter?"

"The picture on my desk? Yes, that's them. How do you know about my wife and daughter?"

"Trish told me."

"Ah Trish, of course." I looked over my shoulder at the silver-framed snapshot on my desk. Dark-haired Nancy, white teeth lighting up the suburbs, on the backyard swing with Jody in her lap. Jody holding a kid-sized football in her hand, by the laces the way daddy taught her. Her mouth is open wide and she is shrieking some tyrannical command at me. I felt the vestigial stirrings of the old heartache and turned away. "It's my *ex*-wife," I said.

"I mean ex-wife. Where are they now?"

"In Fort Worth."

"Do you...?"

"Send them all my money? Yes."

"No," she laughed. "Do you see them?"

"Yes, every few months I try to get down there. I also get Jody summers and Christmas week." I closed my eyes, it seemed for only a second and felt my mind flooded by the memory of the child's last embrace, arms and legs wrapped around me so tightly that it took two stewardesses to pry her off me. To walk away from the plane last December was about the hardest thing I'd ever had to do.

"I'm sorry, does all this make you uncomfortable?"

"Somewhat," I admitted. I got to my feet aimlessly, looking for a way to divert the conversation. "Hey, you hungry?"

I don't think she was but she understood what had prompted the question. "Yes, why don't we make dinner? I'll help you."

We went into the kitchen and assembled the makings of a quick meal, bacon and cheese omelets, my special garlic English muffins, and my patented coffee. The kitchen was small and the constant bumping of bodies eroded much of our constraint. By the time we had the meal prepared, we were almost completely relaxed. We set the table, lit some candles, stacked some Billie Holidays on the hi-fi, and sat down to eat.

I don't know why, but I felt a strong need to tell her how it had happened, the thing with Nancy, and I began to talk, looking first into the hypnotically flickering candles, then into her green, empathy-filled eyes. "It was my third year at Dallas," I said. "I was just coming into my own. My rookie year had been so-so, my second, I was fourth in the league in receptions. Then in my third year..." I closed my eyes and tried to bring the scene into focus, feeling anxiety mount as if it were about to happen all over again, not just the splintered ankle but the splintered life that followed it as well.

"You don't have to..." Sondra said.

"No, it's all right. In my third year I was really burning up the league. Probably would have led it, too."

"What happened? I know you were injured."

I laughed. "Injured? Darlin', I was dee-stroyed." I poured myself a cup of coffee and lit a cigar. "It was the sixth game, against St. Louis. It's the third quarter. We're down by a field goal. We have the ball on their 38, third and three. Don Meredith, you know who he is?"

"Yes, of course."

"Well, he sends me on a tight slant, between the middle linebacker and the strong-side linebacker. Do you follow this?" I arranged some silverware and saltshakers on the table.

"Yes. We watch a lot of football."

"Okay. Now it seems that the Cardinals' middle linebacker, an animal by the name of Larry Wilson, has been coming up fast on inside handoffs. So Don is going to make Larry come up by faking a handoff to one of our backs, Don Perkins. That'll freeze Larry long enough for me to get behind him. Only trouble is, Larry, who's wilier'n a mama bear, doesn't buy the fake. He sees me coming across and drops back to pick me up. To make things worse, Don throws high and behind me. I gotta tell you, I made one helluva catch, but as soon as I went up for the ball I knew Larry was about to give me his best shot."

I closed my eyes again and replayed it for maybe the thousandth time. I'm high in the air, stretched to the limits of my frame. I've spun around to the left to catch the pass behind me and my ankles are twisted around each other like a ballet dancer's. I know Larry is going to roll-block me ankle-high but what can I do? I'm completely exposed, extended like an acrobat hanging by his thumbs. But these things happen so goddam fast. The bolt of agony as my ankles are riveted together by the force of the tackle. The world revolves 270 degrees. The sky rolls away and I see the stadium upside-down.

My ankles, still locked together, one of them already a jumble of shards, are the first thing to strike the semi-frozen turf. A second explosion of agony. A third as the safety falls on them. And all I can think to do is look to see if I still have the football. I find it still tucked in my arms. I laugh! Then I cry. Then I pass out.

"God," Sondra gasped, stuffing her napkin in her mouth.

"That's all right. I probably only had seven or eight good seasons left anyway," I laughed.

Sondra didn't laugh with me. "What happened then?"

"Well, the croakers did a pretty good job with my foot, considering the X rays looked like a jigsaw puzzle before it comes out of the can. The thing is, it's not the same ankle I went into the Cardinal game with and it never will be. It still aches on damp days and when I kick my clients out of my office. Coach Landry said he thought I could rehabilitate it with hard work, but I don't think either of us believed we could ever really put Humpty-Dumpty together again. But even if we did, I might always..."

"Hear footsteps?"

"Hey! You do know your football!"

"So, what did you do?"

"Do? I started my own rehabilitation program. One pint of bourbon a day the first six months, increased to two a day the next six months. Alcoholism is a proud old tradition in the Bolt dynasty and I was determined my daddy wouldn't be the last drunkard in the line."

"And your wife…?

"I don't have to draw you any pictures," I said. It came out as a growl but I didn't apologize. "Let's just say everything went to hell in a hand basket. When I started beating up on her, she started thinking about getting out, when I started beating up on Jody, she decided it was time. Her moving out just made things worse. I got frantic and began drinking my weight daily. I started drifting and every once in a while I'd wake up to find myself washing dishes in Tulsa or hitching in Wichita or puking in Needles, Arizona. Somewhere in there I signed some divorce papers. I was one very busted-up human being."

I looked down and found her hand enclosed in mine. She had not tried to pull away and when I released her she held on, gazing at me with tear-rimmed eyes that flickered in the candlelight.

"This wasn't supposed to be a tearjerker," I laughed nervously.

"What happened after that?"

"What happened after that was Roy Lescade, bless his heart. That's my assho... my tight buddy from school days. He was working for a Dallas newspaper and took it upon himself to track me down. Partly because he thought there was a good story in it but partly out of love, too. Love is what makes Roy such a good reporter. It's also why he'll never be a great one."

"I don't follow you."

"Well," I explained, "he finally caught up with me in Taos, New Mex. I was drunker'n a grizzly at cider time. We had a happy reunion and he says, 'Thunder Bolt, I know where we can get the world's potentest booze and all you can drink free.' I said, 'lead me to it.' So he took me up into the hills and sat me down on a mountain overlooking—you know Taos?"

"No."

"It's got to be the most beautiful spot on earth even the hippies and the coal interests couldn't ruin it. Anyway, I'm sitting there looking out over the valley but it's just one big blur to me. I say, 'Okay, Roy, where's that booze?' And he sweeps the valley with his hand and says, 'There it is. Isn't it intoxicating?' And then he quotes a poem: 'I taste a liquor never brewed in tankards scooped of pearl.'"

Sondra smiled. "That's Emily Dickinson."

"Right. I say, 'Roy, I don't know about tankards scooped of pearl but if I don't have a belt of Old Granddad, I'm gonna come out flailing.' He says, 'Go ahead.' I took a few whacks at him but I was so pie-eyed I just passed out.

"I came to next day, sober and ornery, and he wouldn't let me within sniffing distance of a liquor bottle. We spent a month together, fighting every day, getting that monkey off my back—I was his prisoner. Then one day he says, 'You know what?' I say, 'What?' He says, 'You whipped me today for the first time. You're getting stronger.' And so I was. Another month and I was restored, He took me back to Dallas to live with him. He stuck to me like a Siamese twin until he felt I could be trusted not to resume my dissolute ways."

"Obviously, you didn't."

"It was the toughest job I've ever had to do but I held. He made me eat properly, work out, rest up and keep myself busy. After a stretch I was in good shape. Not good enough to play football again, mind you, but to take my rightful place again in society, as they say. Roy brought me around to Clint Murchison, the owner of the Dallas Cowboys, and persuaded him to give me a job in the Cowboys' front office. I did that for a couple of years and one thing led to another and I went into agenting. And today, I'm sober, respectable, and poorer than a church mouse on welfare."

As I talked I listened to myself and thought, *how easy I'm making it sound, how painless when I summarize it in a few sentences.* Absent was the agony of innumerable temptations to give up and sink back into the euphoria of alcohol. Absent was the sense of the appalling waste of time and energy and money and hope on an act, attenuated over two years, of pure self-destruction. Absent was the heartbreak of realization that I had thrown away all that was dearest to me. Now, in the telling, all this was just dry biographical fact lightened with a few jokes. Somewhere along the way, the feeling had gone out of it and it was now, like my injury itself, a healed wound that throbbed worse on some days than it did on others.

"One day, a few years ago, someone offered me a drink," I said to Sondra. "I downed it and thanked him and walked away and it wasn't until that night that I realized I'd taken a drink. The craving was gone. I didn't hate myself anymore. I could take booze or leave it. I was a grown-up. But now I ask myself, grown up for what? Shoot, grown-up and a buck fifty will get you into the unreserved seats at Shea Stadium."

Sondra gazed at me for a long minute, then got up and kissed me. Not passionately, just—I don't know, understandingly, appreciatively, something like that. We held it for a long time. I made no attempt to follow it up with an embrace—it wasn't a sexual kiss.

I got up and walked around the room feeling a strange turbulence in my stomach. There'd been a lot of girls since Nancy but only a couple that had meant more to me than Fuck and Forget and the signals pulsating in my brain told me Sondra was definitely earmarked Serious Business. If I chose to make it so, at least.

"You never explained about Roy Lescade," she said to my turned back.

"Roy, yes? Well Roy never wrote the story."

"The story about you?"

"Uh-huh. He felt it would hurt me. He felt that no matter how sensitively he handled it, people would always think of me as a former stumblebum. Now that might get me a lot of sympathy but it would also get me a lot of distrust. People would be afraid to hire me, deal with me, work with me, care for me—marry me. Oh, a few inside people know about my past but that's not the same thing."

"Roy sounds like a good man."

"I owe Roy my life. Plus some good stories to make up for the one he never wrote."

I gazed out my window and watched the car lights gliding over the Triboro Bridge like two endless trains, a white one for cars coming at me, a red one for cars fleeing the city. My back was still turned to Sondra and I was reluctant to look at her. I guess I was fearful that when I faced her I would see that she didn't care. Or maybe, even worse, I would see that she did.

The cool, tender hand on my neck answered the question. I pivoted and Sondra was there, her body close to mine, her face raised for a kiss, eyes shut and lips full and moist and faintly parted. My arms slid around her slim waist and hers around my neck. I drew her tight to me and kissed her, this time with desire, my tongue thrusting into the sweet recesses of her mouth where it twined with her own tongue. Beneath the thinness of her dress, I could feel her small firm breasts, the dainty swell of her abdomen, the warm junction of her thighs. I felt myself hardening.

She did not pull away with maidenly modesty. On the contrary, she responded with a gentle rotation of her pelvis. We held the kiss for a long time, our bodies separated from the act of love only by the gauge of our clothing.

I took her hand and led her into my bedroom. She stood before me calmly if a bit shyly, waiting for me to guide her. I reached behind her and unzipped her dress. She wriggled her shoulders and it felt to her feet. Her breasts were high and tip-tilted, her dark nipples erect with anticipation. I kissed them gently and she shuddered. I removed her panties and she stepped out of them and stood before me in the deep shadow of early evening, unashamed and ready. I knew then that she wasn't a virgin, but I also knew she was far from experienced; she was, I suppose you might say, a student.

I stripped out of my clothes and faced her, letting her study me. She ran her hand over my chest, then down until it encircled my hard erection. She nodded almost imperceptibly and lay down on my bed, arms beckoning and legs parted. I kneeled between her knees and looked into her eyes, hoping to express to her how much more this meant to me than a roll in the sack. Her eyes acknowledged the message, then closed. I slid into her and she moaned softly.

CHAPTER X
••••

Sondra wanted to spend the night with me but the Sadler family's affairs were tangled enough without her disappearing too. I made her get dressed, put her in a taxi shortly after midnight, then returned upstairs to sack out. The bed was still rumpled and the sheets exuded the faint aroma of her perfume and the pungent odor of female musk. I fell asleep at once and dreamed I was married to Sondra and Richie was our son. Then the dream turned wicked and I was haunted by the specters of Richie in a ditch with his head cut off, my daughter wandering onto the runway of Kennedy Airport, Warnell Slakey taking a pipe to my ankles...

I hauled myself out of the nightmare at 7, went out for a head-clearing jog along the East River esplanade, then came home and showered. By then it was almost 9. I phoned the commissioner's office but he still hadn't heard anything more from Vreel. He was getting nervous, however, and asked me if perhaps we shouldn't bring the FBI into it after all. I said let's give it another day.

I made a few more phone calls, catching up on the previous day's business, then phoned the Crispus Attucks High

School in Harlem and asked the gal in the principal's office to please locate Reggie McLaughlin and have him call me back as soon as possible. Five minutes later he called.

Reggie was the school's phys ed teacher and basketball coach and a good friend of mine. Several years ago, someone told me he played a terrific game. He was in the famous Ruckers tournament, the annual basketball competition held up at 155th Street and Eighth Avenue in Harlem. I went. He was an exciting player to watch, lithe and quick with big hands and springy legs. I was introduced to him and we talked about my helping him get a college scholarship. But the Army put in its bid first. They drafted him and sent him to a place called Vietnam. One day on a mountain patrol his platoon walked into an ambush and Reggie bought a round of AK-47 in the kneecap. Another flower cut down by the century's stupidest war.

Between excellent medical care and Reggie's own obdurate will, he'd managed to rehabilitate himself to 95 percent of his former prowess. But as I could very well testify, that other 5 percent was the edge that separates the professional sheep from the hopeful lambs. There was no way Reggie McLaughlin was going to make it as a pro. With government aid, he got a phys ed degree at a junior college and I helped him get the coaching job at Attucks High.

"How you been, Reggie?"

"Okay, Dave. You?"

"Takin' care of business. Say, I got a favor to ask of you. You gonna be around in an hour?"

"Sure. Where am I gonna go?"

"Okay, I'll be dropping by the school. Can you round up your best basketball players?"

There was a puzzled silence. "You recruitin', Dave? I don't allow recruiters near my kids."

"No, nothing like that, Reg, but believe me, it's very important. I'll explain when I get up there."

"Okay. See you in an hour."

I called Roy Lescade and asked him to meet me in front of the school in an hour. Then I phoned Trish and told her I wouldn't be coming in again this morning. She called me some new names I'd never heard and hung up with a resounding slam.

I left the building and caught the Lexington Avenue subway up to 125th Street, then walked over to 128th and Lenox Avenue. The first huge drops of a late-spring thunderstorm were spattering the littered pavement and I found Roy Lescade in his wrinkled raincoat pacing outside the front steps. "Why don't you get a new raincoat?" I said to him. "Yours is 100 percent absorbent." Every drop that landed on it spread into a nickel-sized black blot.

"If I did, I'd have nothin' to bitch about when it rains," he said. "Say, what's all this about?"

"I'll tell you in a minute. Here comes the rain."

The pelting rain hit us just as we were trotting up the steps. We ducked inside and Roy said, "Look at this fuckin' raincoat, will you?" It looked like a towel that had just been hauled out of a swimming pool.

We slid into a frenzied, raucous tide of black kids joking about the sudden downpour as they changed classes. We followed the arrows to the principal's office, where a beefy old-timer made out passes allowing us to visit the gym. I was sure she thought we were cops.

"I visited Timmie Lee last night," Roy said.

"How is he?"

Roy pressed his lips together. "I don't think he's gonna make it. And your friend Tatum—"

"I know about Tatum," I said.

The unsmiling secretary gave us our passes and directed us to the gym. Attucks was a brand-new school but despite some vandal-proofing innovations it was already beginning to show the handiwork of the world's most prolific young artists. The gym, however, a bright, spacious, well-equipped one, was totally free of graffiti, as if it were the one place the kids revered too highly to desecrate.

I caught Reggie's eye in the far corner as he worked with a class on the rings. Nearby a group of gangly boys was playing half-court three-on-three, and the quality of the game was high. I studied the players as Reggie trotted over. Compulsively, I glanced at his right knee and noted the criss-cross of scar tissue where the croakers had put his patella back together. Reggie's face was chocolate brown, round, and serious.

I introduced him to Roy. Then I asked him if he'd ever heard of Warnell Slakey.

Reggie's gentle eyes hardened. "I sure have."

"What do you know about him?"

"I know that if I ever find that cocksucker within a hundred yards of this school I'm gonna cut his balls off. I told him so, too. Did you hear what happened the other night? There's this kid Timmie Lee—"

"That's why we're here, Reggie," I said. "I want to nail Slakey for that little episode. I think you can help me. Roy here, who works for the *Post,* is going to cover the story."

"You just say how I can help, Dave. Whatever you need, you got it."

I glanced over at the game in progress. "We need a decoy, a first-rate prospect we can use for bait."

"I dig it, I dig it," Reggie chuckled.

"But the kid can't just be a good ballplayer. He's got to be a good actor, too. And he's got to have balls, because this might be a little dangerous."

"Yes, yes," Reggie said, rubbing his goatee. We watched the game for a couple of minutes. The kids were all over 6 feet tall, fast and aggressive, but one of them stood out. He was almost as tall as I am, thin but hard-muscled, and ferocious in action. He could leap to the top of the backboard and knew all the schoolyard tricks like "pinning" the ball to the board or slamming the rim so hard it vibrated an opponent's shot out of the hoop.

"That's Mike Amos," Reggie said, "He's pro stuff for a certainty. Reminds me of Connie Hawkins."

He blew his whistle and the game stopped abruptly. "Hey, Frisbee! C'mere." He turned to us and said, "They call him 'Frisbee' on account of he hangs in the air for so long."

Mike Amos left the game reluctantly and trotted over. He had a neat natural Afro with big, Clyde-like sideburns. His eyes were suspicious and his expression ultra-cool but when Reggie introduced us his manner softened a little. "You the agent, right?"

"Right."

He grimaced. "Uh, I wasn't really givin' it my best out there. Just foolin' around, like."

"Your 'foolin' around' looks pretty good to me," I said.

Reggie interrupted. "Mr. Bolt isn't here to scout you, Mike."

"No?" he said, a little bewildered, looking from Roy to me.

"It's true I'm not here to scout you, Mike but if you need any help when you're ready to apply to college, you let me know. Meanwhile, I was wondering if you'd like to help us on a kind of special deal."

That perked him up. "Sure!" he said.

"Don't say yes till you've heard what it it's about. There's likely to be some personal danger involved—and you might get hurt."

"Sheeit," he laughed. "I risk my life every time I go to the A&P."

I liked him. "You know who Warnell Slakey is?"

"Uh huh. He hung around our schoolyard till Coach chased him away. Chased him good, too," he said, grinning at the memory. I would like to have witnessed that little encounter. "You know about Timmie Lee?" he said turning serious.

"What happened to Timmie Lee is what brought us here," Roy told him.

"You need help getting back at Slakey, you come to the right cat," Frisbee said. He looked at Reggie. "Remember what you told us that day? You told us, 'Boys, if you got to choose between Slakey and a drug-pusher, you take the pusher.' I didn't understand that until I heard about Timmie."

I felt Mike was right for the part of the eager but naive schoolyard basketball virtuoso dying to be discovered. I laid my proposition on him and he got a faraway look in his eyes, like a budding actor hearing he's up for a lead in a Broadway production.

I wasn't even finished when he said, "I'll do it."

"Maybe you ought to talk it over with your folks," I said.

"My folks haven't told me what to do since I was 6," he said. "If Coach thinks it's all right, I'm ready to go."

Reggie still looked a little dubious, mainly, I think, because of the danger to Mike. Roy said, "Reggie, if we can nail Slakey in *flagrante delicto,* we can wipe him off the streets for years."

Reggie reflected a little longer, then said, "I don't know about any *delicto* shit but I do know I want that guy's ass." He looked at his protege.

"That's all *I* need to know," Frisbee shrugged. "Now, how we gonna work this?"

CHAPTER XI

• • • •

The rain had abated and the sun was breaking through high clouds when I got back to my office and 42nd Street had that steamy translucence that reminded me of a long-lens movie shot that makes everything look shimmery and unreal. I had a gut feeling that something ominous had happened and one look at Trish told me I was right. She sat round-shouldered at the desk, chin in hands, staring vacantly at her work.

"All right," I said, "first, the bad news."

She finally looked up. "It's hard to say what's good news and what's bad. The bad news is, Timmie Lee died this morning. But from what Tatum told me, Timmie was probably better off dead. So maybe that's good news."

I searched within myself for an emotion. It wasn't really sorrow, because I didn't know Timmie very well. And it wasn't anger, because I'd expended that already. What I felt was a kind of disgust, disgust for the senseless waste. You bring a human being into the world and you nurture him and sacrifice for him and invest your love in him and you see him flowering into something of value, something unique and useful, something that promises to reward you and perhaps even achieve some modicum of glory and bring honor to you and invest your life with a little meaning. And then some scum comes along and kills it and pisses on it. This is a waste of such magnitude, it's tantamount to tragedy. I felt so disgusted I wanted to throw up.

"God," Trish sighed as if she'd read my thoughts, "what a fucked-up world this is."

"How much money do we have in checking?" I asked.

"Enough to pay our salaries for the next half hour."

"How about the emergency fund?"

"About two thousand."

"Send a check for the whole thing up by messenger to Tatum and tell him it's for the funeral. And tell him Roy'll be in touch with him today about a plan."

"A plan?"

"He'll understand. Oh—and find out when the services are and tell Tatum I'll be there. Now, what's the good news?"

"The commissioner called. Stanley Vreel has heard from the kidnappers. I guess you can call that good news. Anyway, the commissioner is on his way over."

"Did he say...?"

Before I could finish the sentence the door opened and Commissioner Lauritzen strode in. He was faultlessly attired, as always but his face was pasty and drawn and I detected more than a trace of alcohol on his breath. I'm the last person to criticize a man for drinking in a crisis but goddamn, there's something indecent about doing it before one o'clock.

"Can we go into your office?" he said clamping my hand briefly, more for support than anything else and marching past me like a zombie. I followed him into my office, closed the door behind us, and opened the liquor cabinet. "Maybe just a little one," the commissioner said. I fixed him a big one. I poured myself some club soda.

The commissioner gulped half his drink down and said, "Stanley Vreel heard from them a little while ago. They gave him instructions."

"What are they?"

"They want Vreel to bring the money up to some place in Connecticut."

"When?"

"Tomorrow morning."

"Where exactly?"

"Some place called Macedonia. You ever heard of it? It's in the western part of the state. Near the New York line. Here, I've got it all written down." He pulled a leather-bound notebook and gold pencil out of his jacket and read me the instructions. They sounded like something out of *Treasure Island:* Vreel was to drive nine-tenths of a mile into Macedonia State Park, where he'd find a picnic table, then he was to walk sixty paces north till he came to a certain tree. He was to leave the money under it and return to New York immediately. If he did this, Richie would be released that afternoon. There were to be no tricks—or else.

I jotted down the instructions. "What are you going to do, Commissioner?"

"I want to stake the spot out tomorrow."

"They said no tricks," I reminded him.

"I think we can do it unobtrusively. You know Bo Bowen?"

"Bo? Sure. Guard, Detroit Pistons, 1968 through 1972."

"Good memory, Dave. Bo is an electronics expert. He does jobs for me. He told me it's standard procedure in kidnapping cases to plant a tiny transmitter in with the ransom money. Then the FBI is equipped with these receivers and they can track the guy with the money for miles. Bo is rounding up the gear now. We can have our people planted in a wide perimeter around the drop so the bastards can't detect us."

"That's fine but what about the guys that are holding Richie? Suppose they've been instructed to shoot Richie if they don't hear from their confederates by a certain time?"

"We're not going to capture the men on the spot," the commissioner explained. "We're going to follow them to their hideout."

I went over the plan in my mind and shrugged. "I guess it's as good a strategy as any I can think of. Is there anything you want me to do?"

"Yes. Do you have any plans for the rest of the day?"

"No sir. I've been keeping myself open."

"Good. I want you to drive up there at once and scout out every inch of that area. I want to know the layout around the drop. I want to know about paths and access roads, escape routes, the whole bit."

"Okay. Meanwhile, there's something you can do for me." What's that?"

"It's gonna sound strange, but can you have a couple of your people follow Mr. and Mrs. Sadler today?"

"Mr. and Mrs.—Richie's parents?" He looked into his glass as if a genie had just risen out of the booze.

"Uh huh. Sondra says her father goes out some days and doesn't say where. Her mom supposedly goes shopping. I think we should check up on them."

"But what possible connection...? Well, why not? It's no more crazy than the rest of this thing." He helped himself to one for the road and left.

I gave Trish some instructions for the afternoon and was about to leave the office when I decided it would be nice to have Sondra for company. I called the St. Regis and she answered. Her voice was husky and sensual. "Hello, Dave.

I was just thinking about you."

"Reviewing last night?"

"Yes. I get all squirmy when I think about it."

"Would you like to spend the afternoon with me?"

"Very much," she murmured.

"Be under the canopy on the 55th Street side in half an hour, I'll pick you up."

"What are we going to do?"

"What would you like to do?"

She answered this with heavy breathing.

"What else would you like to do?" I said.

I taxied to the Pavilion and picked up my Camaro in the garage, drove down Second Avenue to 55th Street, and pulled up at the St. Regis. Sondra was waiting, looking shamelessly sexy in a kind of mock tennis outfit with a pleated white skirt and halter-top. Her bare midriff and long, tapered legs turned a dozen heads as she dashed in front of the car and hopped in.

As we pulled into traffic inching toward the West Side, a curtain of discomfort seemed to descend between us. It was odd but as intimate as we'd been a scant 12 hours earlier, we really didn't know each other well enough for the sort of familiarities long-time lovers bestow on each other, the hello kiss or the teasing banter. I think she was wondering whether I was still interested in her after my "conquest." I was wondering if she was mad at me for certain things I'd done with her which, in the bright light of the morning after, might make a nice girl like her feel a little unclean.

She sat leaning against her door and I hunched over the wheel stealing peeks at her tanned legs as if I'd never seen them before.

"Where are we going?" she asked.

"Connecticut."

"I assume you haven't heard from the kidnappers."

"We have. That's why we're going to Connecticut."

She spun around as if yanked. "Are we going to get Richie?"

"No, we're going to the place where the kidnappers want us to drop off the ransom money. The drop is set for tomorrow and the commissioner warns me to check the area out."

"Are you going to try to capture them?"

"Something like that."

"What if...?"

"We're trying to cover every contingency," I said. "Richie's safety is the prime consideration."

She lapsed into a nervous silence and I turned on the radio. We got on the Henry Hudson Parkway at 57th Street, heading north and listened to rock for half an hour as we drove along the stately Saw Mill River Parkway. Just before the highway widened into route 684, Sondra finally broke the silence with, "Why do I feel like a stranger with you?"

"Maybe because you don't know anything about me."

"Yes. Yes. I'd have thought that, um..."

"Last night? What did last night tell you about me? That I'm good in bed, that's all."

She slumped lower in her seat, embarrassed. Another ten minutes passed before she said, "Well, who *are* you, masked man?"

I laughed. "That's 35 years you're asking about."

"We have time."

"Not for all of it, but I can run some highlights past you." I told her my pedigree, going back to Northumberland and including the family crest. And I told her about my Texas boyhood, which had been divided between the ranch and the house in town. The result had been a young man divided. I loved the ranch, knew every inch of it by the time I was 6 and had mastered every task before I was 10. But I also loved the house in Fort Worth, with its fine library of leather-bound books dating back to the seventeenth century. When I got to high school, I was the best-read kid in my class and my teachers started talking about grooming me for a classical education at an Eastern school. At the same time, my daddy started talking about my taking over the ranch.

"And you?" Sondra said. "Which did you prefer?"

"I preferred football," I said. "And baseball and track and basketball and just about every other sport. And, to the dismay of all these folks who had some plan or another for my future career, I was a good athlete."

"Trish says they used to call you Sleeper."

"Sleeper, that was me."

"A sleeper's a player who lets the other team think he's not very good, right?"

"Right. Then, when they're off guard, he burns 'em."

She looked at me and seemed to be sizing me up. "You don't strike me as a sleeper." Then she clapped her hand over her mouth, embarrassed again. "I wasn't referring to last night."

"It never crossed my mind that you were," I said, fibbing. "See, in high school I was kind of rangy and uncoordinated. I moved like a marionette, arms and legs jerking every which way. People tended to underestimate me. Then I grew up and filled out."

Sondra reached out and touched my arm, sending goosebumps up it. "You're still like that a little, I'm afraid. I underestimated you at first."

"That's not hard to do," I said.

Just before Pawling, N.Y. we picked up 22 North. The countryside opened up like a panorama and we skirted some spectacular farmland. I talked about how I'd won all my letters and graduated with high honors and was inundated with sports scholarship offers. For, as Sondra well knew, the combination of athletic prowess and scholastic achievement turns college recruiters on like a bottleful of greenies. I chose the University of Texas, where I could play the best brand of football the nation has to offer but keep my hand in literature as well as take courses in ranch administration. The first, I did well enough to set one or two records that still stand, the second, well enough to graduate magna cum laude.

I looked at Sondra. "You impressed?"

"Shouldn't I be?"

I shrugged. "Sometimes I think it doesn't amount to a pile of buffalo chips. Anyway, I found myself drafted by the NFL, the AFL, the New York Mets and the Detroit Tigers on account of I was also a pretty good catcher, by a basketball team that had never seen me play but figured I must be good at it, plus I had a boxing promoter tell me I could be the greatest white hope since Gentleman Jim Corbett."

"So you joined the Dallas Cowboys?"

"No, I joined the Army."

Her eyebrows flew up. "Sleeper strikes again!"

"I had the Army obligation hanging over my head anyway, so what the hell. But the real reason was, I just didn't feel I was mature enough to decide what I wanted to do with my life. So I joined up. Best decision I ever made, too. Nothing like the Army for postponing decisions. Did my hitch, saw as much of Germany as a Texas boy might want to see, and led my division to a football title. Got my discharge, went home, told my daddy sorry, it was still football, and dropped in on Coach Landry and asked him if he was still interested in me. The rest you know. Still feel like a stranger?"

I could feel the shimmering green eyes fixed on me, and it was hard to concentrate on driving. "No," she said, "I feel like . . ."

"Like what?"

"Like making love."

She placed her hand on my thigh, and suddenly my vision blurred so badly the narrow ribbon of route 22 seemed to expand into an eight-lane superhighway. I swerved onto a dirt shoulder and braked to a skidding halt.

"Darlin', that's an evil thing to do to a man while he's driving."

"I really want you, Dave." She slid her arms around my neck and drew me to her. Her lips were pliant and hungry and her body electric with desire for a repeat performance of last night, right there with tractor-trailers whizzing by so close the car shuddered like a dinghy in a gale. Last night's shyness was gone, replaced by a predatory lust and a need that were awesome. I didn't know what to do, with God and everybody watching, but my hands were way ahead of my mind and had glided beneath her halter to envelop the roundness of her breasts. But I was uneasy about the publicness of the thing. I kept glancing in the mirror, expecting a police car to stop at any moment. In fact, some distance back, a green car was pulling onto the shoulder. Probably a coincidence, but that was enough for me. With the utmost reluctance, I disengaged. "Business before pleasure."

Panting, she pulled her halter down over her breasts and brushed the hair out of her eyes. "Yes, you're right. I'm sorry."

"Maybe when this is all over..."

She looked at me intensely and I realized she may have heard more in that remark than I'd meant to convey. I left the sentence dangling and wondered how to complete it. I cared a great deal for Sondra, cared more for her, I think, than anyone since Nancy. But when I thought of the emotional investment, the responsibilities, the complications of a serious affair—well, I'd have to make very sure before I let the thing go deeper.

And so would Sondra. She'd fallen for me, okay, but what did I really mean to her? Her first big love affair? Her brother's rescuer? An exciting adventure in a lonely city? She'd have to sort it all out. I slammed the gearshift lever into "Drive" and crunched back onto 22 in a shower of gravel.

It was awkward-silence-time again. We stewed in our separate juices as I pushed north on 22 until we picked up 55 a little beyond the Harlem Valley State Hospital. A few minutes later we crossed into Connecticut and picked up route 7, pushing north again along a particularly picturesque stretch of the broad Housatonic River bordered by rolling green hills. About ten minutes later we entered Kent, Connecticut.

The instructions were to make a left at the town's only traffic light but I drove on into town and stopped at a stationery store, where I picked up a map of the area. Then we doubled back to the light and proceeded along Macedonia Road which skirted the grounds of Kent School. Pretty soon we got to the entrance of Macedonia State Park.

I made a mental note of the mileage figures on the dashboard odometer and inched the car over the park's narrow dirt road, which paralleled a rock-strewn stream flanked by campsites and picnic benches. There were not many people in the park so early in the season but nevertheless, we studied every face carefully, wondering if any masked the knowledge of Richie Sadler's whereabouts.

I pulled over for a minute and we studied both the map and the kidnappers' instructions. The road we were on rose into the hills at a gentle grade, then emerged at the other end of the park and linked up with a number of local roads. I tentatively penciled in "X's" at what I thought were the best spots to place our men on the following day. The coverage seemed sadly inadequate considering the sprawling nature of the area but the transmitter gadget the commissioner had told me about might even up the odds a little.

I drove at idling speed, watching the odometer until the numbered gauge at the extreme right indicated we'd come nine-tenths of a mile. I stopped and looked around. We were at the foot of a little wooden bridge just wide enough for an automobile. It veered off the main road to a campsite and we were supposed to drive over it and park. We did and got out of the car.

Still following the instructions, we located the last picnic table and measured off sixty paces north through matted underbrush. The last few paces brought us to a huge old silver birch tree, its bark stripped for kindling and scarred with initials. This was the tree where Stanley Vreel was supposed to leave the satchel containing three million dollars.

I peered through the dappled woods. The tangle was thick, making both mobility and visibility difficult beyond a twenty-five-yard range. I waded as far into it as I could, looking for a path but found none. Unless these guys were skilled woodsmen, they'd probably have to use the main road for entry and exit which was an advantage for our side.

As I paused to get my bearings, I heard the gravel-crunching approach of a slow-cruising car. At first, I thought it was probably just a Winnebago full of campers but then I heard it stop near the bridge and I had the heart-stopping feeling that someone was watching us. I peered through the brush and thought I detected a metallic green glint. I shouted to Sondra to get back to the car fast and I plunged through the thicket toward the campsite, cursing the stubborn, clinging brush that slowed me down. Suddenly there was a wild spinning of tires on dirt and the rattling of pebbles against fender guards. By the time I got out of the clearing, there was nothing but a cloud of dust.

I hopped into the car and wheeled it around furiously. Sondra sprang out onto the clearing and jumped into the car beside me. I gunned the engine and we zoomed over the bridge, following the orange haze of dust that still hung over the main road. A minute or two later we reached the exit of the park—where the road forked. I swore.

"Pick one," I said angrily.

"Left."

"Luck be a lady," I said roaring left. We hurtled down a winding road and followed it for 15 minutes. Then we came to a four-corner intersection. I slammed on the brakes and thumped the steering wheel in disgust.

Sondra looked at me apologetically. "I hope I'm luckier in love," she said.

CHAPTER XII

....

I dropped Sondra off at the St. Regis and parked my car in a nearby garage. Then I walked over to 666 Fifth Avenue, where the commissioner had scheduled a meeting to brief his task force on Project Big Silver Birch, or whatever you wish to call it.

When I walked into the commissioner's office I got my big surprise of the day. There were Mickey MacGuire, Dennis Whittie, Arnie Fried, Red Lipsett, Monty Babbidge, Bo Bowen—10 or 12 retired basketball stars who had faded into obscurity so fast you'd have thought they'd been dropped collectively into the sea. "Je-sus, it's Old-Timers Day!" I whooped, shaking their hands. "I thought you guys had all gone on to the big postgame show in the sky."

The commissioner smiled. "This is what I call my shadow government, Dave. We keep them on retainer for special, discreet assignments."

"Only half of us is shadows," said Monty Babbidge. "The rest is honkies."

We reminisced for a few minutes until Stanley Vreel arrived, looking pale and tense. Then the commissioner called for order. "The purpose of this meeting is to devise a strategy for tomorrow's operation," he said. "Dave Bolt has just returned from the area where the money is to be dropped and he'll brief you on the layout."

I stood and looked bleakly at the commissioner. "Well sir, after I tell you what happened today, you may want to call the whole thing off."

He bit his lip. "What happened?"

"I was followed, that's what."

"By whom?"

"I didn't see him but I think we can assume it was one of the kidnappers." I told them about the car that had followed me. "Unless I miss my guess, Mr. Vreel should be getting a call saying the deal is off. They know I've been scouting the location. They'd have to be pretty dumb not to know why."

The commissioner lowered himself wearily into his big chair and looked around the room with lifeless eyes. "Any bright ideas?"

Vreel waved his cigar. "Aren't we jumping to conclusions?" He looked at me. "Bolt, you say you pulled off Route 22 and this green car behind you pulled off too. Then you continued on to Macedonia but you have no idea whether that green car was still tailing you. Then you're in the woods and you hear a car pull up near the campsite. You look through the deep woods and you *think* you see a green car. The car takes off before you can get a good look at it or even see for sure what color it is. Now, I'll admit that looks suspicious but for all we know the whole thing was a coincidence. So I think that unless we hear from the kidnappers, we ought to go through with our plan."

The ensuing comments indicated general concurrence with Vreel's view and I had to admit it made sense. Up to a point. I said, "Mr. Vreel has made a good case that perhaps I misconstrued the whole thing. It may be that I'm just extra jumpy these days."

I asked everybody to gather around the map I'd marked off and we assigned stakeout spots to each man. Then Bo Bowen, the electronics expert, demonstrated this transponder gadget, a little black box designed to pick up impulses transmitted by a bleeper concealed with the money. He opened a carton and distributed one to each man, showing us how to set it at the proper frequency. Then we went into the strategy part and hashed out every contingency until we were as well rehearsed as the cast of a Broadway musical. The commissioner then broke out the booze. I went into Connie's office and made photocopies of the map.

When I returned, Dennis Whittie took me by the elbow. Dennis, a wiry tall black dude, had been a ferocious backcourt scrapper for the Virginia Squires until he dislocated his hip in a collision with Al Fields of the New York Nets in a playoff game a couple of years ago. The last I'd heard, Dennis was working in a clothing store in Miami. "Aren't you curious about Mr. and Mrs. Sadler?" he said.

"Christ, I forgot all about them! Did you follow them?"

"I followed him, Lipsett followed her. You want a rundown?"

"Is it interesting?"

"Depends on what you mean by interesting."

He took out a note pad and read from it. "At 11:15 AM Mrs. Sadler appeared in the lobby of the St. Regis and Red followed her out. Her first stop was Bonwit Teller, Fifth Avenue and 56th Street. She went to the Lingerie department and bought a blue nylon peignoir. Then she went to Bergdorf Goodman, Fifth Avenue and—"

"Okay, okay. Is that all she did, go to department stores?"

"She went to the Russian Tea Room for lunch and had *blin-*

is. Afterward she went to the powder room and made wee wee."

"Red saw her making wee wee?" I said with a straight face.

For a second Dennis thought I was serious, then he laughed. "Anyway, that's all she did, shop."

"Well, there's nothing criminal about that."

"If my wife spent money the way that lady did, I'd call it criminal," Dennis remarked.

"You followed Davis Sadler?"

"Yeah, and *that's* what I'd call interesting. He came down around noon and had lunch in the hotel. Then he split, walking east to Lexington Avenue. He went past 58th, walked to 59th, then doubled back past 58th, like he was scouting something out. He kept looking behind him, too. Finally, he took another crack at 58th but this time he turned up it."

"Where'd he go?"

Dennis gave a kind of congested chuckle. "Into a rap parlor."

"A what?"

"A rap parlor. They've taken the place of massage parlors. The cops busted massage parlors like crazy about six months ago, after Mayor Beame's wife got indignant. So everybody cooled it for a few weeks, then reopened as rap parlors. Now instead of going in for a massage, you go in for a rap. You pick out a chick, go into a private room with her, get undressed, and talk."

"Just talk?"

He shrugged. "The girls are good talkers. After a few minutes of rap, the customers want to go to bed with them. It would appear that while his wife's out shopping, Davis Sadler's out wenching."

I turned this revelation over in my mind. "It sounds like the logical thing a visiting insurance salesman from the Midwest would do, especially if he's married to a woman like the one Sadler is married to. Except that I'm not sure

Sadler is the kind of man to cheat on his wife."

"You mean there's another kind of man?" Dennis said.

"True. But do you think a man would go alley-catting around at a time like this, when his son...?"

Dennis pondered. "Life goes on, Dave. Whatever a man's troubles, he still got to dip his wick."

"You're probably right," I said but a doubt lingered. I'd started to walk away when a very wild notion came into my head. "Hey, Dennis?"

"Yo?"

"Suppose Sadler doesn't go to this rap parlor to get laid."

"You think he actually goes there to rap?" He issued that strangulated chuckle again. "He'd be the first man in history."

"No, I was thinking maybe he's got Richie there."

"You're out of your gourd."

"Probably, but—you got any plans this evening?"

Dennis backed away, gesticulating wildly. "No, but my wife does. She has this plan not to cut my balls off with a carving knife as long as I remain faithful to her."

"Aw, Dennis, come on, you don't have to actually *do* anything. We'll just have a look around and maybe—well, rap with the chicks a little, that's all."

He shook his head and glowered at me. Then a subtle smile spread across his face. "Mmm—it *is* in the line of duty, after all."

"Right on."

The meeting broke up and Dennis and I walked out into a hazy spring night that glowed purple in the glare of the city's lights. Occasionally the sky crackled blue with heat lightning but it didn't feel like rain. I remembered the morning's downpour but it seemed like a month ago and I suddenly felt incredibly tired. I also realized I hadn't eaten for about 12 hours.

"Do you mind if we stop for a quick bite?" I said.

"There'll be plenty to eat where we're going," Dennis smirked.

"Yeah, but I meant food."

We stopped at a stand-up pizza joint on Lexington. I had two squares of Sicilian and a grape drink. "You know how I think we ought to work this?" I said between munches.

"Mff?" Dennis had a slice of the regular with sausage and peppers jammed into his cheek.

"I think we ought to say we're cops."

"Mff," Dennis shrugged, which I took to be agreement.

I felt a little less light-headed as we walked up Lexington to 58th Street and turned left. About halfway up the block, next to a movie theater, was a doorway with a hand-printed sign advertising the "Communal Encounter Rap Parlor." We squeezed through a long line of kids waiting to see a new Truffaut movie and some of them snickered as we entered the doorway.

We trudged up the stairs, following the arrows. We passed a pink-faced traveling-salesman type on the way down, who slid past us with averted eyes, and came to a landing with a bright red door that was partially open. We entered a small, garishly decorated anteroom with rust-colored walls hung with challis-patterned velvet. The ceiling was draped in brown satin. The sofa, unoccupied, was upholstered in brown plush and the floor was covered with a soft ocher carpet with a phony Persian design.

Facing us was a white desk of simple stamped plastic. The girl behind it was anything but plastic, however. She was a willowy, walnut-colored chick whose furry natural constituted the bulk of her attire. The rest was a satin bikini filled with big breasts and wide hips. Her smile flashed promises all over the place.

"Hi," she said, "I'm Melanie. Can I help you?"

Gazing at the nubs of her nipples outlined against the flimsy fabric of her bikini top, it was hard to remember what we there for but I assumed a stern face, flashed my wallet, and said, "I'm Mr. Bolt and this is Mr. Whittie. FBI."

I was counting on her not looking at the wallet since the card I was flashing was my season pass to the Jet's games. She didn't even glance at it but twisted her lips and said, "I'll get the manager."

She went into a curtained room behind her and emerged a minute later with an extremely wide gent wearing a Hawaiian shirt, a chestful of amulets and sharks' teeth and ivory hands with various fingers extended—and a scowl. His hair was plastered back in a kind of duck's-ass pompadour. He looked like he should have been a Steak-'n'-Shake carhop twenty years ago.

"What's this shit?" he growled. The friendly sort.

"It's like the lady told you," I said.

He looked us over. We were big enough, clean-cut enough, and looked dumb enough to be federal agents. "My dues are paid up," he said, which I took to be a reference to the local police.

"This is federal business," I said.

"Meaning what?"

"I said it was federal business, porky, not your business."

He smiled a sordid little smile. "Look, boys, if it's just a little nooky you want, we do that all the time for our friends down at New York's Finest."

"We might take you up on that, pal, but right now we'll be satisfied with a look around."

"Help yourselves. Just don't go busting into the rooms. I mean, at least wait till the customers are through."

"We don't have time for that," Dennis said.

Porky inflated his chest and stepped in our path. "You got a warrant?"

"Yeah," I said. "Dennis, show him the warrant."

Dennis brought his knee up and caught the poor bastard in the cubes. I'd never heard a guy's nuts crack before but so help me, that's the sound they made. Porky made this pathetic braying sound as he sank to his knees. Dennis looked at me and shrugged apologetically, then dragged Porky, still trumpeting like a ruptured bull elephant, into his office, yanked the phone out of the wall and tied him up with the phone cord.

I looked at him admiringly. "Christ, where'd you learn that?"

"Mostly playing against the Kentucky Colonels," he said. "Never could get to the playoffs any other way."

Nub-nippled Melanie was standing against the wall with her fist in her mouth and several hennaed female heads were poking through a gap in a curtain to our right. "What's this, a bust?" one of them chirped.

I walked over to her and poked her in the tit. "No, *this* is a bust, sugar. How much do you charge to rap?"

She was a frizzy-haired broad, plump and blotchy-skinned and distinctly not my type. She looked at Melanie, then back at me. "Twenty-five dollars for 15 minutes. You want to rap longer, it's another twenty-five for every quarter-hour or part thereof."

"Is there a mileage charge, too, sister?" Dennis asked Melanie.

The fear started to drain from Melanie's face and she looked Dennis over as a potential rapper. "It depends on how far you want to go. You want to ride around the world, you can't get out of here for less than a yard."

"Look," I said, reaching for my billfold, "we're looking

for someone. Let us stick our heads in the doors and we'll pay you for your trouble."

"And if I don't?" Melanie said resigned to the inevitable.

"Then we'll huff and we'll puff," I said. I laid a hundred dollars on her palm and gestured to Dennis to do the same.

"Come with me," she said. The girls crowding around the curtain backed away and retreated into a kind of parlor. They were all scantily clad and most of them were awful, ranging from plucked chicken types to over-inflated pool-float replicas.

"I seen better in Amarillo and that's a vile town," I said to, Dennis.

"You see who you're looking for?" Melanie asked.

"We're not looking for a woman," I said.

She squinted at me. "We don't run *that* kind of place."

"Just show us the rooms," I said.

We passed through a door at the back of the parlor and stepped into a narrow corridor lined with corrugated vinyl doors with latches on them. We paused at the first door. I've done a few weird things in my life, but this came close to copping the giant-sized fruit cake. We listened and heard low muttering sounds. I took a deep breath, shrugged, flipped the latch and looked in.

It was a windowless room, maybe 8 by 10, painted canary yellow and lit by a dim floor lamp in one corner. It had a tiny alcove with a toilet and sink. The air was pungent with the cloying aroma of grass, plus a smell nowhere as agreeable.

Against the far wall there was a bed occupied by a young naked couple sitting facing each other in the lotus position. Their hair was equally long and their chests equally flat and for a moment it was hard to say which was male and which female. It didn't matter, except academically. What did matter was that neither was Richie Sadler. "Oops!" I said, backing out. "Sorry, kids. Thought this was my room."

They looked at me through bleary eyes.

I slid the door closed and glared at Melanie. "What the hell kind of rap parlor is this, anyway? Those people were rapping."

She smiled. "Maybe you'll have better luck in here." She gestured at the next door.

It sounded that way. A baritone voice was grunting something that came out, "Yumm, yumm, yumm." Melanie drew the door back herself, and if we'd been perverts we'd sure have been in luck. In the darkness it was almost impossible to sort out what we were looking at, for there seemed to be arms where the legs should have been, and vice versa. Then I realized we were looking at what the Elizabethans called The Beast With Two Backs. It also had two heads, one at each end.

Melanie boldly switched on the light and two figures disengaged with one mighty frightened leap. The man, a pink little shrimp, was definitely not Richie. The girl, a flabby number with pendulous boobs, hissed, "Get out of here, you cocksuckers."

We apologized and retreated in confusion. Then I got sore and whipped open the corrugated door again. "Listen, sweetheart, you're not really one to call somebody else a cocksucker."

Dennis yanked me back and hauled me down to the next room. "Your turn," I told him.

He wrinkled his face. "If Krafft-Ebing could see me now," he sighed, sliding the door open. I looked over his shoulder and for a second, I thought we'd struck pay dirt. A long, sandy-haired youth was astride a redhead, the prettiest gal I'd seen so far in this chamber of horrors. In the frail light, her lover could have been Richie. His head darted around and he stopped in mid-stroke. It wasn't Richie.

The girl looked at him. "What's the matter?"

"There's someone here."

She stared at us. "You cops?"

"Uh uh," Dennis said. "Just walked into the wrong room. Don't mind us, folks."

She shrugged. "Stick around and watch if you want to." She gazed up at her john. "Finish me," she sighed, squirming beneath him.

He looked uncomfortably in our direction. "I've never done it in front of anybody."

"Forget about them. Just fuck me." She grabbed his ass and pulled him down hard on top of her. For a few moments he was torn between private pleasure and public exposure, but the girl reached around and tickled his balls and helped him make up his mind. Soon he was banging away at her like a lumberman who's just had his tot of rum. He was hung with one fine big rammer, and though they say hookers aren't supposed to feel anything, her heavy panting sounded pretty authentic to me. Dennis began to back out, but I edged him back into the room. "I'm really enjoying this," I whispered.

It lasted another minute or so, his long strokes quickening and the couple's sighs and murmurs and grunts and groans rising in volume until it sounded like Marshall, Paige, Larsen and Eller working out on the blocking sleds. To tell the truth, though I've done as much balling as the next dude, I'd never watched anyone else that close up, except in fraternity skin flicks. I was amazed, for instance, that anyone with a tool that long could work it so damned fast. He finally came with a long wolf-like howl, and if she was faking her orgasm, she should soon replace Helen Hayes as First Lady of the Theater. Her body virtually lifted all two hundred pounds of this cat off the bed, her eyes rolled, her breasts heaved and her tongue rolled around her lips. She said things to him that I haven't heard since boot camp, and after another frantic minute or two of post-coital wriggling, he collapsed heavily on top of her.

She turned to us, panting in flute-like wheezes. "How was that, boys?"

"If he has a hook shot, sign him," Dennis said as we backed out and slid the door shut.

I won't detail the rest of our tour. Suffice it to say it was your standard rap-parlor survey, a lot of people running through the basic 15-minute rap and a few taking overtime with some interesting variations. The long and short of it was that Richie was not there, and Richie's father apparently went there for the very best of reasons—to get fucked and sucked like any other red-blooded butter-and-egg man.

All that bearing witness had instilled a strong desire in Dennis and me to try the merchandise ourselves. Dennis asked Melanie herself, who by this time had warmed considerably to his cool line of jive and went willingly to room No. 3 for a roll in the kip with him. I didn't see anybody who really turned me on, but I finally settled for a doe-eyed teen-ager who hadn't quite yet acquired the hard gloss of a mature hooker, though in all other respects she was thoroughly professional. She was also an excellent judge, telling me I was the very best she'd ever gone to bed with, oh yes indeed.

CHAPTER XIII
• • • •

I was so bloody bushed when I got home I think I fell asleep brushing my teeth. For a change I slept soundly, unmolested by the bogeys that had tormented me the last couple of nights. But this solid rest was to be short-lived. The morrow arrived at the particularly gruesome hour of 5 AM with the jangle of my telephone. How long it had been ringing I don't know, but I knew it was trouble. The commissioner had arranged for his task force to be awakened at 6:30. This wasn't any 6:30.

"Bolt?" It was a strange voice, a contrived voice, a voice deeper than it was supposed to be.

"Armpf," I recall myself replying.

"You want Richie Sadler back?"

"Yeah, but at a decent hour," I said.

"Get a pencil and paper."

I put the phone down and creaked out of bed, went to the sink and dashed some cold water on my face. Then I got a pad and pencil. My movements were automatic but my mind was quickly passing out of the fog. By the time I returned to the telephone I was alert and the juices were beginning to flow.

"What'd you say your name was?"

"No bullshit, Bolt. You do like I tell you and you'll have Richie back by noon."

I gritted my teeth. There was a timbre in that stagy voice that I thought I recognized but I couldn't place it. "Go ahead."

"You know where Montauk is?"

"Yop."

"All right, you're gonna bring the dough out there, starting the minute I hang up. I'll be timing you, and if you're so much as 10 minutes later than I think you should take, it's goodbye Richie. I don't want you settin' up no traps."

"It's gonna take me a little while to get the money, my friend. I mean, it's not lying around on my dresser, you understand."

He paused to think about that. "All right. But no tricks. Try to fuck me and I'll mail Richie's brains back to you in a baggie. Just you and the money, Bolt."

Then he gave me instructions for a drop underneath a boardwalk on a beach at the eastern end of Long Island, outside a town called Amagansett. Then he rang off.

I hung fire before calling the commissioner. Something was wrong, something weird. Why had the guy called *me?* Up to now, he'd been calling Stanley Vreel. I pressed my temples to squeeze an explanation out but it wouldn't drop. I phoned Niles Lauritzen at home.

"Dave? Hi, I just tried to get you and your line was busy."

"You tried to get *me?*

"Yes. Stanley Vreel just called. As you suspected, the kidnappers have called the drop off. They know you were up in Connecticut yesterday checking the place out."

I could hardly speak. "But Mr. Lauritzen, I just *got a* call from the kidnappers. I'm supposed to drive out to Amagansett right away to drop the money out there!"

There was a long, flustered silence. "Either these guys are brilliant or their left hand doesn't know what their right is doing."

"Or there's two sets of kidnappers."

"Two sets? But there's only one Richie Sadler."

"Look, Mr. Lauritzen, I don't understand it any better'n you but this guy wants his money in two hours and he sounded very sincere. Can we get it pronto?"

"I've got to go to the safe in my office. I can be there in 10 minutes."

"See you then."

I climbed into a pair of blue jeans, boots, and a polo shirt and grabbed a sweater in case it was cold out at the beach. I was about to leave when I remembered that transponder gadget Bo Bowen had issued me. I found it on my coffee table and took it along, forgoing my shave and my coffee.

I took the elevator down to the garage and roared out in the Camaro feeling uglier than a warthog in menopause, mostly because I'd been deprived of my shave and coffee. I don't pamper myself much but those two things are my *sine qua non* for getting the day off on the right foot. Take them away from me and I'm a very hostile lad. When I played for the Cowboys, I never drank coffee or shaved the day of a game. By game time, I was so fucking mean I was ready to break telephone poles over my knee.

It was pitch dark at 5:15 as I drove up to Fifth Avenue and down to 666 at 53rd Street. At that hour even New York's famed night people are in bed. But there were four cars in front of the building. I pulled up and saw Dennis Whittie. He ran over to the car.

"Morning, Dave. Any symptoms of the clap yet?"

"Not yet. What're you people doing here?"

He looked puzzled. "Why, the commissioner called and

said there'd been a change of plans, that we were going to follow you out to Long Island."

"Ah." I'd forgotten to tell the commissioner the kidnapper's warning that this must be a one-man operation, but a moment later he came out of the building, lugging a big sack with the help of Red Lipsett and Stanley Vreel. I got out and opened the trunk and we dumped the sack in. "Commissioner..."

"You got that whatsamajigg?" he said.

"It's in the car." We hunched over my front seat and turned on the transponder. It issued a sharp beep and two seconds later another. I turned it off. "Looks good, but commissioner, this guy told me just me and the money. If they see your all-pro panzer division, we're gonna blow this gig and maybe get Richie killed. Now, I think I can track this cat on my own, then contact you when he's led me—"

"Uh uh," the commissioner said. "We're coming with you."

"But commissioner..." I started to argue, then looked past him to Stanley Vreel. Vreel was looking at me with suspicion written all over his face. Suddenly I understood what was going on. "Commissioner, you don't think I concocted this story, do you? You don't think that I...?"

"We'll be a safe distance behind you, Dave," he said.

I looked at Vreel and mentally called him a truly terrible name. Then I cut out.

The fastest way to the Long Island Expressway from midtown is via the Queensboro Bridge. With the lights of four other cars strung out behind me, I took off over the upper roadway and once in Queens, weaved along the approach to the Expressway. I was really furious with Stanley Vreel for putting a bug in the commissioner's ear that I had made up the story about a phone call from the kidnappers and was going to hijack the ransom money myself. I was also furious with the kidnappers for denying me a good night's sleep, my shave and my coffee. I turned on the radio and all I could get at that hour was news and Latin music and that just made me madder. The news was bad, as always, and I hate Latin music before 9 AM.

By 7, as the eastern sky started to fill with pearly light and patchy pink clouds scudded over the Atlantic to the south of me, I'd calmed down somewhat. My partners' cars were not far behind me but didn't have to keep in visual contact with me because of the exceeding light traffic. I rolled down the window. It was chilly but the tang of salt air was bracing. The Hamptons, the main body of towns at the tip of Long Island, were beautifully etched in blue night-light as I rolled silently through them. I'd spent a few weekends out here with a girl I used to go with and the memory of one night on the beach with her, under the blankets on the dunes that fringe the Hampton beaches, came back to me vividly, too vividly. I slapped my cheeks to restore meanness. It's a bad idea to go tracking kidnappers with a hard on.

The last town in the Hampton string was Amagansett, a colony of arty looking but expensive beach houses scattered at odd angles like toys kicked by a kid. I turned right onto the dirt road and drove slowly through the colony. Many of the houses were deserted, Memorial Day weekend, which traditionally kicked off summer, was still weeks away. A month from now, at least on weekends, the joint would be hopping with more free pussy than a convict's daydream.

I came to a chain marking the frontier of civilization, as we know it. I could hear but not see the beach since the view was blocked by low rolling dunes tufted with scrubby grass. A few hundred yards west, however, where the dunes rose to a crumbly palisade, was a notch covered by a boardwalk, a kind of mini tunnel through which bathers not intrepid enough to scramble over the dunes walked to get to the beach. It was there that I'd been instructed to leave the money.

I hauled the big post office canvas bag out of the trunk of the Camaro. It was heavy as a bitch and I wondered why the commissioner hadn't been able to come up with anything bigger than fives, ones, and rolls of quarters. At least it felt that way but then I'd never hefted three million dollars before. I half-carried and haft-dragged the sack down to the tunnel and found a hollowed-out timber in the wall supporting one of the dirt sides. I jammed the sack in there, then paused to listen and look. I heard no sound but the surf and saw no sight but the seagulls and terns wheeling around the froth looking for washed-up clams, dead fish, and the usual mung sea birds eat. My flesh felt creepy because I knew I was being watched but by whom and from where I didn't know. My orders were to drop the sack and get back in my car and go.

I returned to the car and went.

I drove a hundred yards down Montauk Highway and parked. Then I dashed into a little grove of mangy trees behind the colony until I came up on the dunes, several hundred yards east of the drop, and started slithering back along the boardwalk. I was in good shape but I hadn't done this sort of thing since basic training at Fort Sam Houston.

That put me in mind of the fact that I didn't even have a weapon. I'd rushed out of the house without arming myself with so much as a hatpin. Fuckin' sons of bitches who wake you up at 5 and make you rush-ass out of the house without a shave and coffee.

After what seemed like miles of lizarding over the dunes, I came to a halt about 25 yards away from the trestle. I hunkered down so that my head would not be silhouetted against the horizon and searched the four points of the compass for a sign of my antagonists. I was rewarded only with a glimpse of a pair of gulls who hovered over me, concluded I was neither fish nor garbage and veered off to the sea for a more appetizing morsel.

It wasn't particularly cold, yet I was so hungry, tense, and caffeine deprived that I began to shiver and twitch as I squatted on the planks waiting for something to happen. Ten minutes passed before something did, during which time the sun palely rimmed the eastern horizon. I cursed it because it brought no heat but as I was the highest point in Amagansett it must have illuminated me like the Statue of Liberty at daybreak. I flattened myself against the plank walk and as I did I saw my man.

He was a short, thin figure, a man I could easily take were it not for the object that glinted purple in his right hand. He wore a heavy dark sweater and a wool mariner's cap and he'd been waiting almost directly underneath me at the foot of the palisade, on the beach. He moved in jerky, mouse-like spurts, like a Walt Disney cartoon figure, pausing cautiously to sniff the wind for danger. I hugged the boardwalk and made like I was scenery. I watched him pause at the entrance to the tunnel and peer in stealthily. From the way he never looked back I was fairly certain he was alone; if he'd had a confederate, he would have signaled him. Still, I scanned every tussock of grass for signs of another person. If there was one and I didn't see him, the male lineage of the Bolt dynasty would come to a halt in about 2 minutes.

Satisfied that he was alone, I crept up to the trestle and peered through the cracks in the planks. There he was, pulling random packets of bills out of the bag to make sure the ransom hadn't been padded with newspaper. Then he pulled the cords of the satchel tight.

I was not too happy, to say the least, about his having a gun and my being unarmed but I figured there was no time like that moment to make my move, preoccupied as he was with his triumph. I rolled off the trestle and swung down, aiming my boots for the hand bearing the gun. They connected and the gun went off. The report was thunderous and not just because we were in a tunnel. It must have been one helluva big gun, a sawed-off shotgun or a .45. My hearing became a high dial tone.

But that wasn't the worst of it. The worst part was that I'd failed to kick the gun out of his hand. I can testify to this because the man brought it down on my cheekbone, not enough to put me down but more than enough to check me momentarily. My head lit up with starlight but I reasoned that at least he'd chosen slugging me over putting a slug in me. I think he thought I was going under because he relaxed to watch me stagger. I darted out a hand and grabbed the wrist with the gun and shook it like a riata. The gun spun out of his hand and while he reached for it with his other hand I got a lick in with my left fist, a good cross to his temple.

Unfortunately, it was the only lick I got in. The next thing I felt was this volcanic pain in my testicles where his knee had connected. I heard myself groan. I tried not to lose contact but that's easier said than done. He pulled loose and snatched up a handful of sand and smacked it into my eyes, rubbing it maliciously. I have no compunctions about fighting dirty but this guy was doing all the things I wanted to do to him, only sooner. I folded up on the sand and there was an eerie pause as if he were groping around for the gun. Obviously, he didn't find it, because he muttered, "Fuckin' shit, fuckin' shit." I guess that frustrated him because he kicked me in the face. Warm ugly blood flowed into my mouth and I hit the sand, arms around my head, waiting for the brain-splintering coup de grace. But it never came.

As I lay on the sand rolling around helplessly, choking and wondering if there were any charitable organizations specifically designed for blind, deaf, and toothless eunuchs, I heard him dragging the sack off, cursing. It was impossible to say for sure with the siren still blaring in my ears but I thought I knew that voice.

I got to my feet as rapidly as my throbbing scrotum permitted and staggered out to the surf. I waded in up to my knees. It was bitterly cold as I scooped up several handfuls of saltwater and washed the sand out of my eyes, ears, nose, and throat. The salinity stung my cheek and gums where my assailant had lacerated them but a cursory tooth-check with my tongue indicated all the little fellows were snug in my jaw where they were supposed to be.

I blinked several times but despite a lot of gritty particles still lodged under my eyelids, I could see all right. I sloshed out of the tide and stumbled back through the tunnel and up to the beach and my car. There was no sign of my quarry but I still had a chance of picking up his trail. I flipped on the transponder and gave off a faint signal. I twiddled a dial the way Bo Bowen had shown us and the directional said "east".

Burning rubber, I dragged onto the Montauk Highway heading toward the town of Montauk. I found myself on a barren stretch of highway about four miles long. The bleeps began to get stronger. The needle on my speedometer swung to 100 miles per hour.

A sign that whipped past indicated I was coming to a fork that divided the Old Montauk Road, which I remembered to be a narrow and winding one that followed the beach, from a new, well-paved blacktop. Here the transponder couldn't help, since both roads went east more or less but I chose the new highway, figuring that if I was wrong, I could reverse my error faster than I could on the poorer road.

Luckily, this time I had chosen the right road. The signal grew so loud I had to turn the volume down on my little black box, a few moments later it reached a crescendo when I zoomed over a hill and whizzed past the town garbage dump on my left. Then it began to fade and I realized I'd overshot. I made a swerving U-turn that would have warmed the heart of a Grand Prix driver and headed back to the garbage dump. The signal was really wailing now, like a Geiger counter in a uranium mine, and it reached deafening proportions as I jounced over the cratered road through a stand of runty pines that opened on an immense landfill overlooking the Long Island Sound.

The place smelled precisely the way garbage dumps are supposed to and no better for belonging to one of the wealthier communities in the country. Overhead, a flock of huge squealing gulls flapped, darkening the morning sky while their brothers lit on everything in sight. I came up behind a parked Caterpillar tractor that blocked my view of the landfill. Then I bounced past it and saw a gratifying sight.

Close to the edge of a plateau, a sort of artificial hill of sand piled on top of inu garbage, sat a green car of recent vintage, encircled by other automobiles including a gray Caddy I recognized as belonging to Mr. Lauritzen. My assailant was stretched over the hood of the green car surrounded by the commissioner, Stanley Vreel, and the gallant men of the American Basketball Association's First Commando Group.

As I coasted down the hill to the plateau, I fixed my eyes on the figure bent so ignominiously over the hood of his car. I simply wanted to confirm what I now had concluded from the memory of his voice and the sight of his car. He looked up as he heard my car approach. I got out and walked up to him.

"Hello, Manny."

"Hello, cocksucker," he spat out. Somewhere along the way, he'd lost his wool cap. His right temple had an egg-sized purple bruise where I'd clipped him. Otherwise, he was the same Ratso-Rizzo looking creature I'd whiled away an unpleasant half-hour with in Queens a few days ago.

Niles Lauritzen came up to me and looked pityingly at a face that must have looked as if its maker had finished it off with O-grade sandpaper.

"Jesus, what did he do to you?"

"Nothing, commissioner. I always look this way before I've had my first cup of coffee. Did you get the money back?"

"Sure. That bleeper worked so well the guy might as well have sent up flares telling us where he was."

"What about Richie? Did he say where Richie is?"

"We're trying to elicit that information now."

Dennis Whittie had Ricci's arm twisted so hard behind his back it was almost touching the nape of his neck. Ricci screamed, "I don't know, I don't know, you fuckin' nigger son of a bitch."

I gestured to Dennis, who gave Manny one last sadistic jerk of the arm for "nigger," then let go. Manny's eyes were flooded with tears of pain. He slowly unbent his arm, rubbed his eyes and wiped his nose with the sleeve of his sweater. Then he looked at me. "I could of killed you back there, you know."

"They'll reduce your sentence by ten years for that," I said. "That'll leave you with eighty-nine to go. Where's Richie?"

"I tell you, I don't know, Bolt. I don't got him. Break my arms, I don't know."

I shrugged. "Dennis, break his arms."

"Wait a minute!" he shrieked. "Wait a minute, listen to me! I didn't snatch the guy."

"Wasn't that you who called me this morning?"

"Yeah, yeah, that was me."

"So?"

"So it was a bullshit story. I don't have the kid and never did."

"Then what's this all about?" Stanley Vreel demanded.

"It's about robbing the ransom money. Hijacking it, you understand?" He looked at me. "After you told me Richie got snatched? Well, I started tailing you."

"Me? What for?"

"Because I figured sooner or later you was gonna walk out of a bank or something carrying a sack full of money. Money to get Richie back with. I'd follow you to where you left it then I'd walk off with it. Now do you see? Buddy, I been your shadow for days. And you never had clue one. At least, not until yesterday."

It made sense, unfortunately. It explained why Ricci had phoned *me* this morning instead of Vreel. If Ricci were the real kidnapper, he'd have known that Vreel was the one to contact. "That was you who followed me up to Connecticut."

"Right. I thought yesterday you was making the drop but I guess you was just taking that broad for a picnic. After you chased me out of the park, I went back and tramped all over those fuckin' woods, but I didn't find the dough. So I drive back to New York and while I'm driving I suddenly realize, Jesus, there's an easier way to hijack the money than tailing Bolt! So I called you and said I was the kidnapper."

I looked at Commissioner Lauritzen. "And just about the time he was calling me, sir, the real kidnapper was calling Vreel to cancel the Connecticut drop. Pure coincidence."

"See?" Manny grinned. "That proves I don't have Richie."

"Yes," Lauritzen breathed, looking like he was going to cry. "But it doesn't prove who does."

CHAPTER XIV

• • • •

It was only midmorning when I returned to my apartment but I felt as if I'd been up since the turn of the century. I showered quickly, sending great eddies of beach sand into the drain, then shaved. Looking into the mirror was an act of sheer masochism. My face looked like the last days of Pompeii. My eyes were a network of ruptured capillaries and I could still feel tiny sand grains under the lids. My lower lip had a long gash in it from where Manny had kicked it into my teeth and both lips were swollen. My cheekbone had a nasty bruise the color of a lemon and almost as large. Small wonder the doorman had gaped at me like something obscene washed up on a beach by a flood tide.

I was ready to kill for a cup of coffee but I didn't have time. I dressed hurriedly and grabbed a taxi to the office, ardently hoping to rehabilitate my business affairs, which had shriveled to a shrunken caricature of their former selves.

Trish almost passed out when she caught sight of my realigned face. "Jesus, where have you been?"

"Down in the dumps. Anybody call?"

"Yeah, but wait a sec and let me do my Florence Nightingale number."

She went to a file cabinet, stretching her pert figure to its utmost to reach a first-aid kit jammed in at the rear. Her tight little ass, smartly encased in thin slacks, and her jersey-clad breasts were a sight for sore eyes and, believe me, I overqualified for the role. She returned and with a great clamor of solicitous noises dabbed the last stubborn grains out of my eyelids with a cotton swab.

"Poor bubby," she murmured, pressing close to me. Her tongue flickered over her lower lip in concentration.

"Is the bump and grind necessary?" I said. "I mean, Marcus Welby doesn't dry-hump *his* patients while he's swabbing their eyes."

"Marcus Welby isn't a specialist. I am. Look up."

I rolled my eyes toward the ceiling and she deftly dipped the swab into my lower lids.

"Who called?" I asked.

"Sondra, for one. She wants to know what's up. What *is* up, anyway?"

"If you don't put some distance between us, you'll find out soon enough."

"Gosh, I'm sorry." She gently rotated her hips and pressed her thighs close to mine. So much for distance. The only thing that went down was my resistance.

"So? What happened this morning?" she asked.

"We thought we had our kidnapper but he turned out to be just another shitass trying to make a dishonest dollar. I'll call Sondra. Who else?"

"Your newspaper friend with the wandering hands, Roy Lescade, to remind you Timmie Lee's funeral is today."

"Oh God, I really need a funeral today. What do you mean, wandering hands? Has he tried anything with you?"

"Only if you call grabbing my boobs and feeling me up trying something."

"That son of a bitch. What time are the services?"

"Noon."

I was hardly up to it, but I felt I should go. "Book me a reservation on the A-train."

She shrugged. "It's your funeral." Her tongue flicked faster as she applied the finishing touches to my face. Her breath was sweet and her perfume heady. She pressed herself against me aggressively and the laughter was rapidly fading from her eyes. She was starting to take the game seriously. So was I.

"There, that about does it. Look up. Now look down. Now to the left. Now right. Now stick out your tongue."

I did and she engulfed it with warm, hungry lips and sucked it like a licorice stick. It almost drove me up the wall and for half a minute I accepted the gambit, curling my tongue around hers and cupping her ass with my hands. But it was no good and for the same old reason; she was more valuable to me as a secretary than as a lay, difficult though it was to order my priorities with an erection. I slid out of her embrace. "I'm sorry, darlin'. The same guy who sandblasted my face also kicked me in the groin and my equipment has to go back to the shop for a few days. If you really want to satisfy my appetites, how about calling down for two burgers, two French fries, and enough coffee to float a Japanese supertanker."

Her body trembled with frustration and she panted like she'd just come off a quarter-mile sprint. "Bastard! He didn't kick you hard enough." She plopped down in her chair, phoned in the order, and started typing like a machine gun. You'd have to say the girl was mad.

I went into my office and phoned Sondra with the bad news that the operation had been called off. I didn't bother to tell her about Manny Ricci. I told her I'd call her later. Then I shuffled some correspondence, dickered a little on the phone, and brooded till Trish came in with a green paper bag with my food order and dropped it on my desk from a prodigious height. I pounced on it like a loose football and glommed it down with obscene murmurs. I belched, sipped my third cup of coffee, and brooded some more. What I brooded about was why the real kidnappers had canceled this morning's drop. Had they, like Manny Ricci, observed me checking out Macedonia Park? There was something important here but I had an awful headache and now I was developing indigestion from having eaten too fast too late— and besides it was 11:30 and I had to leave for the funeral.

I walked west on 42nd Street and caught the subway to 125th. The funeral parlor was on the corner of 126th and Seventh Avenue, around the corner from the Apollo Theater. It was a well-kept little building that stood out among its tatty neighbors as if to remind passers-by that the only way to go first-class in Harlem is to die.

The turnout was impressively large. The parlor where Timmie lay in state was thronged, particularly with kids. There was a lot of laughter and jiving but somehow it didn't sound irreverent. Even Timmie's mother, a sturdy, handsome woman in a black satin dress and pillbox hat with veil, was joshing with some of Timmie's friends. It reminded me of a New Orleans wake I once attended.

This respite from grief was short-lived. The funeral director, a corpulent, grim-faced man in tails, shouldered through the crowd and summoned Timmie's mother, her two little daughters, and the rest of the immediate family to the chapel. The poor woman shuddered and wailed and the hubbub stopped stone-cold as if death itself had trailed its cape over the throng.

As the family filed out, I walked up to the coffin. They'd done a good job of fixing Timmie's face up but I could still see the purple lacerations on his cheeks, chin, and temples beneath the make-up. The kid must have been worked over by Slakey's goons something awful. Timmie's face wore the same frown as the day I'd played ball with him. He was a morose kid and not very sociable but my last memory of him was his coming up to Richie and shaking his hand. At that moment, he'd been bigger than Richie, especially in the light of what Richie had told me afterwards about really having tripped Timmie and intentionally too. I plucked a white carnation from a large floral wreath standing at the head of the coffin and dropped it in the coffin. "I'll see what I can do, Timmie," I said softly. I felt really bad.

I looked around and saw the hulking, slouched figure of Roy draped in that perpetual raincoat of his. He was talking to somebody who, as I sidled up to him, turned out to be Tatum. We shook hands solemnly.

"Thank you for the check," Tatum said.

"Sorry it couldn't be bigger."

"We was just talking about Mike Amos?" Roy said. "We set him up in the schoolyard, you know? Well, Slakey came around to look him over and started hitting him with the agent line?"

"And?"

"Slakey's hooked. They made a deal. Slakey's going around calling Frisbee his protégé and telling everybody Frisbee's the next Oscar Robertson. He told the kid he was contacting several college coaches. For that privilege, Mike paid him five hundred bucks. Which you owe me, pal—I laid it out for him."

"And did Slakey contact those coaches?"

Roy grinned and pulled out a little note pad. "I phoned

Mal Griswold at Ohio State, Connie Chochran at Mizzou, Steve Gray at Stanford, Parker Smith at Cincinnati, Mark Keller at USC, and Ab Stein at Niagara.''

"And? They never heard of Slakey, right?"

"Right." Roy snapped the pad shut. "What's the next move?"

"What do you usually do when you've got a fish hooked, asshole?"

At that moment there was a tremendous commotion around the door and it carried over into the parlor as word traveled about who had just arrived. I peered at the door but the throng was too thick to see anything. Then, as suddenly as the uproar had begun it died down to a hush and the crowd parted. The silence was eerie and the air seemed to crackle with static like the heavy atmosphere before a summer storm. And a moment later I understood why. Warnell Slakey had come to pay his respects.

"There's a man with brass balls," Roy murmured as Slakey, wearing an expensive dark suit, walked arrogantly through the gauntlet of sullen black faces, stepped up to the bier, and looked down at Timmie. I had to agree with Roy, it took what Trish calls "chutzpa" for Slakey to turn his back on that volatile crowd.

Tatum was breathing heavily and I braced for trouble. Roy picked up on it too and put a soothing hand on Tatum's shoulder but Tatum wrenched away, stepped forward and pointed a wrathful finger at Slakey. "Murderer!" He pronounced each syllable with venomous precision.

Slakey was cooler than ice. Aside from his shoulder blades twitching a little, he didn't move. My peripheral vision picked up movement on the fringe of the crowd and I spotted Slakey's bullyboys threading their way to the front of the parlor. The funeral director standing at the back began wringing his hands and a number of mourners began loosening their ties and taking off their glasses. I hadn't been in a good brawl since Dick Modzelewski stuck his finger in Don Meredith's eye in a 1964 Giant game but this one was shaping up to be a doozie. I was sorry as hell when the funeral director shrewdly pushed his way into the center of the crowd trilling, "Everyone into the chapel, please. The services are about to begin." There was a surge toward the door and a promising rumble was nipped in the bud.

We funneled out the door and were just starting for the chapel when Roy nudged me and gestured with his head down the corridor. Mike Amos, half hidden behind a potted palm, was gesticulating at us. Roy, Tatum, and I cut away and walked down the corridor. Mike slipped into the men's room and we followed. "Sorry about the spy stuff," Mike said, leaning against the door so no one else could get in. "I didn't want Slakey to see me frat'nizin' with you."

"What's happenin', son?" Tatum asked.

"Slakey's doin' his UCLA number on me. Says he's got John Wooden interested in me."

"How much is he asking?" I said.

"Another five hundred."

"What'd you tell him?"

"Tol' him it'd take a while to round it up."

I looked at Tatum and Roy but they looked back to me for the initiative. "Okay. I want you to tell Slakey you've changed your mind. Tell him you don't feel he's doing anything to earn his money. Tell him you don't want him for an agent anymore."

Mike looked at me levelly as if my instructions had not registered on him. But his eyes flickered with fear. This was the crunch. This was what he'd volunteered to do. But until now it was just a game. Now it got dangerous and maybe it got deadly.

"Then what?" he asked.

"Then you show up tomorrow morning like you been doing, to play basketball. Hopefully, Slakey and company will come around to have a little discussion with you."

"What are you goin' to do?"

"Let's just say you'll have help. Do what Slakey tells you and leave the rest to me."

Mike shifted his gaze to Tatum as if checking it out with a soul brother. Tatum nodded. Mike said, "Later." We filed out of the bathroom.

We took seats at the rear of the chapel just as the preacher, a weathered, battered, beautiful old gentleman with tightly kinked silver hair, reached the end of his eulogy. "Yes, my friends," he said with one hand resting on the foot of Timmie's coffin, "the death of a youth is a special kind of tragedy. When our elders depart this life for the hereafter, our sorrow is deep, yes, but it is also tempered by resignation, for we are prepared from childhood for the passing of our parents. But who can prepare a mother for the loss of a son? Who can resign a father to the loss of a daughter? Where is the logic, where the justice, where, we ask, the fairness that God should have us bring forth a child on a bed of agony, have us suffer and sacrifice for him that he may grow tall and strong and straight and righteous, and then watch him interred in the prime of his years? Are we not justified in angrily asking God, with Job, 'Is it *good* unto thee that thou should'st oppress, that thou should'st despise the work of thine hands?' *And* because *this* child"—he thumped the coffin with his fist—"because *this* child, Timothy Lewis Lee, was smitten down by a violent hand, is his mother not justified in demanding to know of God, as Job demanded, 'Wherefore do the wicked live, become old, yea are mighty in power?'" He shot a withering glance toward the back of the room.

"NO, BROTHER NO!" the congregation cried out, twisting in their seats to look scornfully at the object of his wrath. Slakey stood leaning defiantly against the doorjamb. I felt Tatum's body, wedged between Roy's and mine, grow taut as a ship's cable in a gale, but he gritted his teeth and turned away.

"...To accept," the preacher was saying quietly. "Nay, not merely accept but praise the Lord and repent, yet again with Job, for doubting of God that *'Thou canst do everything.'* Small consolation, you will say, to offer a bereaved mother. Yet I would have her remember that the selfsame hand that taketh away also giveth. And I would have the sinners among you remember that the selfsame hand that strikes down the innocent also BRINGS DOWN THE WICKED! Let no man leave this room without indicting that lesson on his heart of hearts."

"Amen!" I shouted with the congregation as we stood up for the benediction. I looked over my shoulder for Slakey but he was gone. I wondered if he'd indicted the preacher's last words on his heart of hearts or whether he even had one.

CHAPTER XV

• • • •

I scarcely had a foot in the door when Trish jumped up from her desk, spun me around and pushed me out the door. "The commissioner's office, right away."

"Did he say why?"

"No, but I think this is *it.*"

"It," I muttered hustling to the elevator. I taxied up to 666 Fifth and Connie thumbed me right through to the commissioner's office. Niles was sitting, Vreel pacing, and both looked like men stretched to the snapping point. Their greeting was strained and I noticed they didn't look at me directly as we talked. Of course, there was no love lost between Stanley Vreel and me but I was puzzled by the commissioner's frosty air.

"I heard from the kidnapper again just a little while ago," Vreel said.

"The real one this time, I hope."

"Yes, no doubt about it. He says he's giving us one more chance but he warned me very explicitly, any more funny business and Richie will be murdered."

I looked at the commissioner. "What're we gonna do?"

He heaved such a big sigh, I thought he'd deflate down to a bagful of skin. "We're going to pay the money."

"You mean, without a fight?"

"We can't take the risk. These people seem to know everything we're doing."

"At least put the bleeper..."

"No bleeper," the commissioner said. "Nothing."

I shook my head. "Look, we don't have to do anything elaborate. Just one guy staked out..."

"No," Lauritzen said. "And that's final."

I walked around the room for a minute, too stunned to speak. Then I remembered something I'd been thinking about since that morning. "Commissioner, how did the kidnappers know we were planning a trap this morning?"

He and Vreel exchanged looks. "Maybe they saw you driving around Macedonia Park," the commissioner said. "Or maybe they've got this office bugged and heard our strategy meeting last night."

"Or maybe," Vreel added, fixing me with belligerent, penetrating eyes, "one of us is playing ball with them."

I stepped up to him and eyeballed him right back. "You wouldn't want to say who, would you?"

The commissioner shouldered between us and pushed us apart. "Nobody's saying anything, Dave."

"The fuck he isn't, commissioner. He's saying *I'm* in cahoots with the kidnappers and you know what else? I think you believe him!"

"Dave..."

"Why in the name of creation would I do such a thing?"

"Shit, Bolt," Vreel snapped. "Three million dollars is as much motive as anybody needs."

That was it for me. I pushed the commissioner aside and grabbed Vreel by his $300 lapels. "I suppose I also needed a pistol-whipping and a kick in the nuts and sand rubbed in my eyes?"

The commissioner recovered quickly and tugged at my arms, begging me to let go of Vreel, who I had lifted half off the ground about a foot away from one of the commissioner's picture windows.

"Vreel," I said, "it would take a helluva lot less than three million dollars to motivate me to chuck you out the window to see if you glide. Someone offer me a quarter."

Vreel clawed at my fingers. He was strong but I was mad and it would have taken a crowbar to pry me loose. But the commissioner shouted, "Dave, let him go, that's an order."

I gave Vreel my best hate-stare, then released him with a shove. "Next time you negotiate anything with me, mister, you'd better wear a helmet with a face mask." I turned to Lauritzen. "Commissioner..."

He held up his hands and turned his back, like a referee walking away from an irate manager protesting a close call. "I'm sorry, Dave, but my decision is final. Look at it this way, if all goes well tonight, we'll—"

I didn't hear the rest of it. I just stormed out of his office.

It was too late to go back to my office, so I walked all the way back to my apartment, shedding sparks all the way from 53rd and Fifth to 77th and York. The walk did me a lot of good, however. By the time I got home, my feelings had begun to settle into their proper proportions. I was still angry enough at Vreel to be sorry I hadn't defenestrated him. But beyond that, I felt a curious sense of relief that the ordeal was soon to be over—at least if the kidnappers kept their part of the bargain. Why should I care if they got away with it? It wasn't my three million dollars. All I wanted was my client and my commission.

I remembered I was supposed to call Sondra. I did so as soon as I got upstairs. She was half out of her mind.

"What's going on?" she said stridently. "Why didn't you call me back?"

"I've been at the commissioner's. The operation has been rescheduled for tonight. You should have your brother back before morning."

She covered the phone with her hand and I heard her muffled voice repeating the news to her parents. When she got back on I said, "Can you get away?"

"Yes, yes I'd really like to."

"My place?"

"I'll be there in half an hour."

In a little less than that, she rang the doorbell. I opened the door and she went limp in my arms sobbing uncontrollably as she discharged her pent-up anxiety in great wracking gusts. I held her tight saying dumb things like, "There, there," but they managed to calm her down until her sobs subsided into little hiccoughing whimpers. I picked her up and carried her into the bedroom, undressed her and laid her. It was a simple and straightforward task, almost like changing someone's oil or brewing them a pot of tea. I instinctively felt she didn't need lovemaking so much as relief, emotional relief in the form of physical relief. She came fast and in deep rolling convulsions, like the swells on a vast open sea.

I held her for a long time and might have begun a second time, this time something closer to the act of love, but another mundane appetite drove us out of bed; we were both starving. We dressed and I reserved a table at another favorite restaurant of mine called Once Upon a Stove, down on East 24th Street.

We never got there. In fact, where we ended up was not just another place but another dimension.

It started when I realized I'd forgotten to speak to the commissioner about lending me a couple of his enforcers for the following day's confrontation with the Slakey mob. So I called him at home but his wife said he was still at the office. Of course, I knew what he was doing there; he was preparing to hand that bagful of loot over to Stanley Vreel for delivery to the kidnappers.

The commissioner said he was rushed but he looked up the numbers of Dennis Whittie, Bo Bowen, and Red Lipsett for me and read them off. I thanked him and added, "I'm sorry about that little scene at your office today."

"It's okay, Dave. We're all under a lot of pressure. Stanley feels bad about it too and said he was going to call you tomorrow to apologize."

"But you're still going to pay the ransom without—"

"Yes," he cut me off sharply, "and in fact, I'm supposed to meet Stanley downstairs in five minutes, so if that's all, I'll speak to you later. Don't forget to call me, or have the Sadlers call me, the second Richie turns up."

"Believe me, I will, commissioner."

I hung up and saw that Sondra was looking at me curiously. "What was that 'scene' at the commissioner's office you were referring to?"

"Aw, Vreel got hot and insinuated I was somehow mixed up in your brother's kidnapping. Can you imagine?"

"Why would he think that?"

"Because the kidnappers seem to be hip to everything we're doing. Vreel thought maybe there was a leak and it was coming from me."

She shrugged. "By the same token, it could be coming from him."

"Sure," I said airily, not thinking seriously about her remark, "that kind of thing cuts both—" Suddenly it hit me like a Claymore mine. "Hey, give me that again."

"About Stanley Vreel, you mean? I just said, if information is leaking to the kidnappers, it could just as well be coming from him as from you."

My heart was pumping so fast I twitched like a hound in the final stage of rabies. "Mama get a hammer, there's a fly on daddy's head!" I dived for the phone and called the commissioner's office again, but there was no answer. I grabbed Sondra's hand and raced down the hall with her.

"What is it?" she panted, staring at me.

"Stanley Vreel, that's what it is!" The elevator seemed to take five years to arrive and another ten to descend to the basement. I sprinted to the Camaro and started it swiftly as Sondra leaped into the seat beside me.

"Can you tell me what's going on? Where are we going?"

"We're going to 666 Fifth Avenue," I shouted as we shot out of the garage the instant the automatic door cleared my roof.

"You think Vreel...?"

"I don't know for sure but a lot of things suddenly make sense to me."

I was too busy driving to explain. Not driving, actually, but breaking the law, for I went through red lights at York Avenue, First, Second, Lexington, Park, and Fifth, getting lucky at Third and at Madison. Then I wheeled onto Fifth Avenue and went through so many red lights I was beginning to think they didn't come in any other color.

When I crossed 57th Street I edged the car to the left side of one-way Fifth Avenue and continued cautiously downtown. About halfway down Fifth I saw it and breathed a sigh of relief; the commissioner's gray Caddy was parked in front of 666, surrounded by a little knot of people. The trunk was open and the white post-office satchel was being tossed into it by Vreel, the commissioner, and one other guy that I think may have been Red Lipsett. I parked catty-corner and turned out my lights. A minute later Vreel got into the car and waved goodbye to the others. I turned my lights on again and, using a taxi on my right to shield me from the commissioner standing in front of the building, I pulled into traffic about two blocks behind the Caddy.

At 50th Street Vreel turned left and drove east to First Avenue, then headed uptown to 61st Street, where he picked up the Franklin D. Roosevelt Drive north. I slid into the flow of traffic about five cars behind him and stayed with him at about fifty miles per hour. Sondra chain-smoked five cigarettes.

For the moment I was able to relax and began to reason out loud. "Why not Stanley Vreel?"

"Because he *has* money," Sondra argued.

"Does he? Maybe on paper but when it comes to hard cash, he's no better off than I am, and honey, that's poor. He told me himself he had a cash problem." I stared at the Caddy's taillights and felt my mind starting to churn out connections. "Do you realize he's the only person who's spoken to—or claims to have spoken to—the 'kidnappers'?"

"That's true. He could have been making it all up."

"That day in the commissioner's office, after we packed you up and sent you back to the hotel with Trish? We were conferring, the commissioner and Vreel and me, and Vreel opposed bringing the FBI into it. Oh, he gave us good reasons but maybe what was really on his mind was that his chances of getting away with the kidnapping would be better if there were no FBI and no publicity."

"That makes sense. Since the commissioner was relying on him for advice, he was in a position to manipulate all the commissioner's decisions."

"And mine too." I scratched my cheek. "Of course, he was opposed to paying the ransom, but that could've been an act. He knew that sooner or later, when all else failed, we'd *have* to pay the ransom, so he let the commissioner talk him into going along." I shifted my thoughts to that morning. "He called off this morning's drop because it was too dangerous. With that bleeper gadget stuck with the money, it was impossible for him to finesse the ransom away from us. Then later today, he tells the commissioner the kidnappers called with a new rendezvous plan but there must be absolutely no tricks or Richie is finished. The commissioner asks him what we should do and Vreel, naturally enough, says, 'I think we'd better do what they say because they sounded like they meant business.' "

"And that scene in the commissioner's office today, where he suggested you were collaborating with the kidnappers? That must have been aimed at diverting suspicion from himself," Sondra pointed out.

"That and destroying our last hope of setting another trap."

"But isn't some of that ransom money his own?"

"Some, but not much—maybe one or two hundred thousand and even that was probably advanced to him by the league. No, Vreel stands to make a tidy profit on this deal—certainly enough to pay your brother's bonus."

Sondra lit another cigarette but drew on it less frenetically than the others—more contemplatively, you might say, as if she were struggling with a heavy question. In fact, she started to ask it, but got only as far as, "Dave...?"

"Yes?"

"Oh, nothing."

I didn't pursue it, I suppose because I was afraid to. Because the same question had occurred to me and it raised so many disturbing possibilities, my blood turned icy at the thought.

We were now on the Harlem River Drive and Vreel took the exit lane that linked up with the Cross Bronx

Expressway. I stayed behind him some five hundred yards back. We swung east on the Cross Bronx. A swarm of cars momentarily cut the Caddy off from view and I accelerated to keep up with it. That proved to be a mistake because traffic melted away and I found myself a car's length behind Vreel just as he turned off abruptly onto the Hutchinson River Parkway. I had no choice but to do the same and he could not have failed to notice the maneuver if he was looking for a tail in his rear-view mirror. As I've said, I'm no private eye and this bonehead plan sure as hell proved it.

It also proved Stanley Vreel's undoing, however, because in the next few seconds he unthinkingly tipped his hand. What he did was as soon as he hit the Hutchinson, he swerved off it again gunning the Caddy up the cloverleaf ramp and onto the Cross Bronx Expressway and driving back in the direction from which we'd just come. Up to that moment, I didn't know whether my theory about him was correct or just a crock of high-grade cowshit. I'd figured to follow him until he either dropped the ransom off for the real kidnappers or absconded with it himself. But by trying to shake me after discovering I was tailing him, he told me the answer. For if he were innocent he'd have flagged me down and bawled me out for disobeying the commissioner's orders. Instead, his first impulse was to lose me—the impulse of a man with a guilty conscience.

"Fasten your seat belt," I commanded Sondra as Vreel, realizing he'd blown his cool, pulled away sharply in the hope of shaking me completely. At that hour, around 10:30, the Expressway wasn't crowded and the Caddy pushed up to eighty effortlessly. I kept up with him, praying for a traffic cop to do my dirty work for me but you know what they say about cops when you need them.

I kept him in sight as the lights of the George Washington Bridge loomed up ahead of us. For a moment I thought I'd nail him at the tollbooths, then I remembered that there were no tollbooths, at least not for cars leaving New York for New Jersey. What they'd done was remove those booths, put them up on the inbound side, and doubled the tolls. It still cost drivers one buck to go out and come back but the congestion on the outbound side was eliminated. Consequently, Vreel flashed over the bridge into New Jersey without even hitting his brakes.

A few moments later he veered right onto the Palisades Parkway, a scenic highway paralleling the Hudson River on the New Jersey side. He then hit the throttle full out and if you've never seen a late-model Cadillac accelerating from eighty, you've missed one of the marvels of the Atomic Era. Despite the fact that my foot was almost down to the floorboard, the Caddy simply pulled away from us as though we were standing still.

I took the Camaro up to one hundred but Sondra started making gasping noises and frankly, even I had a slightly woopsy feeling in my diaphragm such as I always get when I forget what my daddy once told me, which is that if God wanted man to break the sound barrier, He'd have created him with rockets up his ass. I decided to try to keep Vreel in sight as best I could at a twenty mile-per-hour disadvantage. I knew he couldn't escape me by speed alone, because at 120 m.p.h. about the only thing you can manage is staying on the highway, to get off, you've got to slow down.

Vreel got around this problem, however, and damn near got us all killed in the process. The road curved to the left abruptly and for a moment he disappeared. I expected to pick up his lights again as soon as the road straightened out but when it did he was nowhere to be seen. At first, I thought he was up ahead around another curve but out of the corner of my eye, I picked up the red glint of a tail reflector and at once realized what he'd done. He'd turned his lights off the instant he entered that curve, braked sharply and skidded onto the broad grass sward bordering the highway, hoping I'd zoom past him. Actually, I did, but a second later I hit the brakes and swerved over the curb. For a second, we were actually airborne and when we finally touched down the wheels clutched nothing but turf. We must have cut a swath slightly longer than the Great Rift.

I'd overshot Vreel but he'd skidded into some bushes and was having difficulty extricating the Caddy. I swung around and raced back before he could get turned around. I blocked his car with the Camaro, flipped off my seat belt and hit the door all at the same instant. I hoped to hell Stanley didn't have a gun but if he did it had better be a big one because I was coming like a rhino with a toothache.

Vreel tumbled out of the door on the passenger side just as I was yanking open the door on the driver's side. I dove across the seat and caught just enough of his heel to trip him up. He fell on the grass with a loud grunt. I scrambled after him, figuring he'd run for it but instead he flipped over and lashed out at me with the same heel I'd just tripped. It caught me in the shoulder and I felt something wrench where my shoulder and left arm join. It was a good shot but no stopper. My right fist itched to express my towering anger, considering all the indignities I'd suffered at this man's hand. I caught him just under the left ear. It was not exactly on target but, like a six-iron to the green, put me an easy putt away. Unfortunately, Vreel folded before I could get a second blow in. He buried his head in his arms and whimpered, "Okay, okay, okay."

I grabbed his shirt and hauled his face close to mine. "Where is he, motherfucker?"

"I got him, I got him, don't worry."

"Where?"

"A motel."

"Take me there."

"I... I can't."

"Can't? CAN'T?" I drew my fist back. "Who's in on this with you?"

"I can't tell you, Bolt. Kill me, I won't tell you."

"It's someone I know, isn't it?"

He looked at me and gave a kind of mocking snort. Then he said, "I'll make a deal with you. I give the dough back, I have Richie released, and you forget about this."

I glared at him. "Forget!"

"You're getting your money and you're getting the kid! Tally it up and it's nothing won, nothing lost."

"Vreel, you're absolutely beyond belief."

He began talking fast, like a salesman pitching high-quality goods and I must admit I could see how he'd managed to talk himself into, or other people out of, several fortunes. "Look, Bolt, use your noodle. Once you tell the commissioner, he's going to have to take some kind of action against me. That's gonna mean publicity. Now maybe I stand to lose the most in terms of reputation but don't you think a lot of other people are gonna look like horses' asses too, including you and the commissioner? Christ, you may end up going to jail for concealing a crime."

"I'm not making any deals with you, Vreel."

"I still have the power to have Richie killed."

"I doubt that very much if your accomplice is who I think he is."

"But you don't know who he is for sure, do you? You think you do—but suppose you're wrong?"

I tried not to show him that he'd scored a point with

that thrust but he picked up my hesitation and followed up hard. "You see, Bolt, I got nothing left to lose any more, so whether Richie lives or dies means shit to me. That ransom money was my last hope against bankruptcy. I needed it to carry me until fall. With Richie as my star attraction next season, I know I could have helped the league nail down a network television contract. But I needed operating capital until then. My credit lines are exhausted, Bolt. My creditors have all but picked my carcass clean. My only other source was the mob and you know what that would have meant."

"You're a man of unimpeachable integrity, Vreel."

"Integrity is all I want to hold onto, Bolt. Let me off the hook. I'll be ruined but at least I'll be able to start again in some other line."

He looked up past me and I realized Sondra was standing over us. "This is your brother's keeper," I said.

"I know. I heard."

"Reason with him, sweetheart," Vreel urged her with a purr. "He wants to turn me in. He does that and your brother will be dead in two hours."

"That's not true," I said.

"My confederate has his orders; if I don't call in by midnight, he's to take Richie out into the woods and shoot him."

I looked at Sondra. "He's lying, Sondra. He's bluffing. Nothing's going to happen to Richie."

I saw her frown in the reflected glow of the Camaro's headlights. "How do you know?"

"Because I know, that's all."

"Tell her, Bolt," Vreel said. "Tell her your cockamamie theory. Tell her who you think my confederate is."

I brought the back of my hand down across his mouth. "Shut up, you bastard!"

His mouth filled with blood and he choked and sputtered but he was relentless. "Tell her, Bolt."

"Tell me what?" Sondra said frantically. "What theory is he talking about? Who do you think his confederate is?"

I looked away from her, away from Vreel, and up into the starlit night. I wished I could be transported to one of those stars, just for a few seconds, so that I could return to earth with this segment of time excised like a malignancy and lost to memory forever.

"I think it's Richie himself," I said.

I looked into Sondra's eyes for a reaction but it was not the one I'd expected, shock. My words didn't strike her sensibilities so much as they were absorbed by them as if she had been somehow prepared as if she'd thought of it herself. This was the question that had hung on her lips in the car, then had been obliterated as too painful to conceive. This was what I had tried desperately to protect her from, yet deep in her heart, in that one corner of objectivity that had not been flooded by her fanatical devotion to her brother, she knew I was right.

But Vreel was the devil himself. "Have you ever heard anything so ridiculous?" he chuckled through a blood-filled throat. He hawked and spit. "Why would Richie allow himself to be kidnapped? For money? For publicity? I mean, you gotta be out of your mind, Bolt."

"How about because he's sick?" I hissed.

"Sick?" Vreel laughed again. "He's the healthiest specimen of young manhood I've ever seen. Where do you come up with this shit, Bolt?" He appealed with his eyes to Sondra.

"Let him talk," Sondra said.

"On the surface," I said, "Richie is Frank Merriwell himself, the All-American boy, every parent's ideal. But way down deep, I think that boy is hurting bad because the pressure to be perfect, to be the greatest ever—nobody's big enough to stand up to it. Something's got to buckle. Forgive me for saying this, Sondra, but I think your father broke Richie somewhere along the line. He makes his decisions for him, what team he's going to play for, how many eggs he's going to have for breakfast, what virtues he's going to be a paragon of, what girls he's going to see or not see. And he's been doing it since Richie was a toddler. That love affair of Richie's you told me about—when your father broke that up, he broke Richie's will as well. What took its place was this insatiable hunger to win and to be perfect. I'm not talking about a winning mentality, now—I'm talking about something pathological."

"Jesus, what crap!" Vreel croaked out.

"I saw it with my own eyes the day I played basketball with Richie," I said. "He fouled a kid intentionally just to keep the other team from winning, then didn't have the guts to own up to it, at least not there. Then later he told me. And he told me how he uses his reputation to build up what did he call them? —'Honesty credits' so that when he finally does cheat at critical moments, no one will believe it. That's how he got away with double-crossing Manny Ricci and making himself a pile of money in the NCAA final. Who's going to take Ricci's word against his? And now this."

"But why?" Sondra pleaded. "He doesn't need the money."

"He doesn't need money per se, but he needs what the money represents—freedom from his father. The trouble is, his father presses him so hard, the only way for Richie to establish independence is by stealing and conning."

"But he must know he'll get caught sooner or later," Sondra said.

"Know? Darling, he *wants* to get caught. He wants to fail. Because in failing, he punishes himself. And in punishing himself, he punishes his father."

I got to my feet and yanked Vreel to his. Sondra stood swaying back and forth like a tree that's just weathered a storm. Vreel opened his mouth to speak to her but I grabbed his cheeks with my right hand and squeezed till his lips looked like a fish's. "You've said enough, you little shit."

I could see Sondra's shoulders twitch several times and I knew she was quietly crying. Then she sucked in a deep breath, turned abruptly, and looked at me with hard eyes, eyes so crystalline and cruel they seemed to belong to someone else.

"Vreel is right, Dave. Your theory is ridiculous."

I gasped. "But you *know*..."

"I know it's almost midnight. We've got to get Vreel to a phone to call his friend and tell him to free Richie. You will do that, won't you, Mr. Vreel? If we promise to say nothing of this to the commissioner?"

"I give you my word."

"Sondra," I begged, "you couldn't be so blind..."

"I think I saw a public phone booth a few miles back," she said tonelessly.

CHAPTER XVI

• • • •

We sat in Georgie's Coffee Shop in 130th Street nibbling on danishes and sipping coffee and watching the action across the street. There was me, my buddy Roy Lescade and Lester Pardee, a black detective from the 28th Precinct who'd been assigned to the Timmie Lee murder case. He was off duty that morning but I'd invited him to join us on what might turn out to be an interesting adventure.

In the playground across the street, a number of half-court basketball games were in progress. One that had attracted a lot of attention was a rugged two-on-two matchup between Tatum Farmer and Bo Bowen on one side and Dennis Whittie and Red Lipsett on the other. A bunch of kids and hoop buffs were lined up on the perimeter of the court, noisily rooting for the old-timers (who were all of 35 or so). It wasn't like when Kareem or Nate Thurmond come around but if you like good basketball there was plenty of it that morning.

In an adjacent court, another game was getting underway, involving younger players. One of them was Mike Amos—"Frisbee".

"That's your sacrificial lamb?" Detective Pardee asked. "He's pretty good, not afraid of contact."

"He's got a basketball career locked if he wants to pursue one," I said.

The detective looked at his watch. "What makes you so sure Slakey's gonna show up?"

I looked at him. He was a big, squarish man with boxy shoulders, large hands and rough features. His hair was straight and shiny, his nose and lips bulbous, and his eyes yellow and mean. He was not the kind of man one fucked around with lightly and I was very glad he was in the employ of the good guys and not the bad.

"I'm not sure but I think he will. If he lets Frisbee off without making him pay, he loses his juice up in Harlem."

He looked at his watch. "It's 10:45 already."

"What's your rush? It's your day off."

"I like to ball on my day off," he grumbled. "Besides, I don't care for this setup very much. It's not an official operation but it's not unofficial either. That's the way people get killed. It also happens to be the way half the crimes around here get solved which is why I agreed to come down. But if somethin' don't happen by 11, I'm gonna split. I got some eatin' pussy biggr'n the Holland Tunnel layin' in my bed, so I sure as hell don't need no cowboys and Indians shit this morning, you dig?"

"Sure, that's fair enough," I said.

The waitress hovered around us with the coffee pot but I covered my cup. I'd needed a lot of coffee to brace me, having gone the night without sleep, but another drop and I'd float away. It had been a busy night which should have ended with the capture of Stanley Vreel but only began with it. A little before midnight, we'd found a telephone and Vreel had called his "confederate" and ordered him to turn Richie loose. Then we drove up to White Plains, Vreel and me in the Camaro and Sondra in the Caddy—I'd transferred the ransom to my own car because I didn't trust *anybody* in the Sadler family anymore—and found Richie where Vreel said we'd find him, in the train station. His hair was mussed and his clothes rumpled but otherwise he looked well treated. He told us all about how this man he'd never seen before forced him into a car and drove him at gunpoint up to a motel where they'd been cooped up all week. His abductor, he said, had a confederate but Richie never saw him—the two conferring only by telephone. When Richie, relating this part of the tale, looked at Vreel, I detected not the faintest indication of collusion between them and believe me I was studying their expressions microscopically. The whole thing was so convincing I really began to doubt my own hypothesis.

We called the Sadlers and the commissioner and drove back to the city for a reunion at the St. Regis at 3 in the morning. I won't go into the story Vreel, Sondra, and I had concocted to explain how we managed to get Richie back without paying the ransom and how I ended up in the picture after the commissioner explicitly ordered me to stay out of it. But it was one of your better yarns and everyone was too happy with the outcome to press for details, at least that night. Vreel was cooler than grandpa's icehouse and we backed each other up so persuasively you could have booked our act for a month at The Sands. Later the commissioner would sit on us for a detailed explanation, he never got one and to this day is still trying to get to the bottom of it though I can tell you he has some beautiful theories.

Anyway, I spent an hour calling my pals Whittie, Bowen, and Lipsett to make arrangements for that morning's little interview with Warnell Slakey. They were delighted to be awakened at 4 or 5 in the morning and told me so in colorful terms. Then I went back to my apartment to catch a little shuteye, except the phone rang at 6. It was Sondra.

"I had to do it, Dave," she said.

"I suppose you did."

"Vreel could have been telling the truth. I couldn't afford to take that chance, no matter how slim it was. And neither could you. Richie is, after all, your client."

"He is that, all right," I said, feeling little joy in the fact.

"We're going home tomorrow evening. I thought I might see you before leave."

"I'll see you off at the airport."

"That's not what I meant."

"I'm afraid I'm going to be occupied," I said.

"I thought you'd say that."

"It happens to be true."

"Dave...?"

"Please, Sondra. You got your brother back. Now you two can live happily ever after."

I pressed my ear to the phone hoping against hope that she'd say something to restore what had been broken but what really was there left for her to say? She'd declared herself loudly and clearly when she pulled the rug out from under me the previous night. "I'll always love you," she said, before hanging up.

I got up and took a long walk along the Carl Schurz Park promenade on the East River, watching the tugboats lug garbage and hoping someone would mug me and put me out of my misery. But some days you can't even find a mugger to work you over. Feeling bluer than ever, I returned to my apartment, showered, shaved, and brewed myself a pot of coffee. All of which helped but I was still feeling pretty evil when I boarded the bus for Harlem.

At 10:55 Slakey showed up. He was dressed, as always, like Pimp of the Year, sporting a white jumpsuit and high-heeled shoes and a hat with a brim so broad you could have run the Millrose Games around it. As he ducked through a ragged hole in the chicken wire fence, he gave the high sign to someone beyond our line of vision and I could easily guess who. Then he strolled casually into the yard.

He spotted Mike Amos and greeted him but walked past the game as if Mike weren't the reason for his visit. He noticed the action in the next court but gave it wide berth when he recognized Tatum Farmer. He ambled over to another corner to rap with some friends.

After another five minutes or so, Mike Amos's game ended and he sat down against the fence dabbing the sweat off his face with the tail of his T-shirt. Across the schoolyard, Slakey pretended to be oblivious but finally waved at Mike and walked over to him. At that same moment, Tatum's game accelerated and ended. The four players walked off the court, toweled up, and popped open some beer cans. Roy, Detective Pardee, and I got up and paid our check.

Slakey was walking around the yard with Mike, gesturing with his hands. In pantomime, it looked friendly enough but it was not hard to imagine the text of Slakey's sermon. Mike eventually shrugged and ducked through the fence escorted by Slakey. The kid glanced in our direction and I nodded reassuringly.

We remained inside the coffee shop, waiting. A minute or so later, four men walked past. They were Slakey's boys. Across the street, Tatum watched them and gave them two or three minutes, then led Dennis, Bo, and Red out into the street. Their group split up, each going his own way, and they trucked innocently down 130th Street, far behind Slakey's men. We left Georgie's and strolled along in the same direction.

At St. Nicholas Avenue, Slakey's people turned right, following their boss to 135th Street, where he turned right again. Tatum's guys trailed raggedly behind and we lagged behind them. By the time we reached 135th Street, Slakey and company were nowhere to be seen, but about halfway down the block, in front of a dilapidated brownstone walkup, Red Lipsett stood with a grin on his face. He saw us and waved us over. He gestured with his head into some shrubs beside the stoop. We looked down and there was one of Slakey's yeggs who, apparently, had been posted as a lookout, sprawled out on his back, out colder than a witch's tit.

"Whose place is this?" I asked the detective.

"Clarence Meddie, one of Slakey's friends."

I looked at Red and he nodded behind him, indicating that the rest of the troop was already inside the building. We went in and huddled at the landing. Dennis Whittie was on the second landing and gestured to us to come up. We tiptoed up a rickety stairway that smelled of wine and urine, then up another flight where Tatum and Bo stood outside a paint-peeled green door with the number 3A. Detective Pardee drew his .38 special and pressed against the door. We crowded around him, straining our ears, but for a minute the dialogue was indistinct. Then the volume began to rise and we heard Slakey say, clear as a bell, "What do you think, I work for nothing?"

"You don't do nothin', you don't get nothin'," Mike Amos replied arrogantly.

"What you mean, 'do nothin'? I been negotiating with a dozen coaches, tops in the country. Now I got a chance to introduce you to John Wooden hisself. I worked my ass off to set this up and I want my money."

"Well, I think you're full of shit," Mike said. He was deliberately provoking him and if I were in the kid's place

I'd have been praying like crazy that my friends were standing on the other side of that door.

"Watch out, boy," Slakey said menacingly.

"What you goin' do, beat it out of me?" said Mike.

"Don't invite me, nigger, I'm too happy to oblige."

"Like you obliged Timmie Lee?"

There was a slap and a cry of pain. We automatically started to rush the door, but Pardee held us back with an upraised hand.

"You sayin' I had anything to do with Timmie Lee?" Slakey said.

"He owed you money, didn't he?" Mike said, sobbing. "He found out what a bullshit artist you are and he refused to pay you. So you had him beat up, right?" There was another slap and Mike whimpered.

"Leave him alone, Clarence," Slakey ordered. Then he said something too low for us to make out.

"*You* say," Mike answered, "but everyone knows you done it."

"Yeah, and I'm still on the street. That should tell you somethin'."

There was a long pause, then Slakey said, "Look, boy, I'm runnin' out of patience. The way I see it you got two choices. You can be a basketball star or you can shuffle-ass the rest of your life on two busted legs. What's it gonna be?"

I had to hand it to Mike. He had no idea whether we were standing outside the door or not. Defy Slakey now and in minutes he could be a cripple or even a cadaver. But he said, "Up your ass, Slakey."

"All right, boys," Slakey said.

Detective Pardee nodded and three of us stepped back and hurled ourselves against the door. It burst open in a shower of splinters, revealing a dismally furnished apartment with chintzy furniture and linoleum floors. Mike Amos was seated in a kitchen chair facing us, his arms held by two thugs. Before him stood Slakey and the one called Clarence, a rubber hose poised. They all staggered backwards with surprise, one of the thugs reaching into his belt for a gun. Detective Pardee rushed him and brought the barrel of his gun down viciously across his face. Tatum was next into the room and made straight for Slakey. He caught him in the gut with his head, like a bull and Slakey doubled over his back with a long groan. They fell into a corner and Tatum laid into him like a madman, cursing him and clobbering him with both fists.

Dennis, Bo, and I hurled ourselves at the other two, while Roy screeched a Rebel yell to spur us on—and took refuge behind a closet door.

Our two brutes recovered quickly from their surprise and traded some solid punches, one of which caught me on the same cheek Manny Ricci had bashed yesterday. That made me mad as hell. I slammed the dude with my elbow, bringing on a red gusher from his nose, while Dennis Whittie kicked him in the groin, which is Dennis's specialty. The other guy had been efficiently taken care of by Bo Bowen and was doubled up on the floor cowering like a whipped dog.

I looked around for more action but the fracas had ended much too quickly. The only remaining action was Tatum Farmer kicking Slakey on the floor trying to make him get up and fight some more. Slakey wasn't having any, which was understandable in view of the fact that a piece of his left ear had been bitten off by Tatum. An ear for a life isn't exactly how the formula goes but I think it worked out pretty nicely anyway.

Detective Pardee finally pulled Tatum away, then called the precinct and asked us to leave before the police arrived because he wanted the credit and vigilante actions don't sit well with precinct commanders. That was fine, though; we'd gotten our vengeance and Roy Lescade had gotten his story. Hopefully, Slakey would get a jail term.

I looked over to Roy, who was scribbling furiously in his notebook. He gazed at me from under his beetling eyebrows and shook his head disgustedly. "Still using your elbows, Bolt. You haven't changed a bit."

CHAPTER XVII
• • • •

A husky female voice announced the departure of their flight and I rose from my seat along with the Sadlers and drifted with them toward the security checkpoint, beyond which visitors were forbidden. Davis Sadler, looking shrunken with worry but happy, shook my hand and I mumbled a platitude to him. I bore him no ill will though it was his ironclad determination to make something transcendent out of Richie that had warped his son so grotesquely. Davis had made Richie 99 percent perfect but in my opinion, people should be a lot less than that, because the remaining 1 percent is too often monstrous. Give me someone 75 percent okay any day, like Roy Lescade, or even 51, like myself.

Bea Sadler, loaded down with so many purchases she looked like she'd hit the jackpot on Let's Make a Deal, bestowed a liquor-laden kiss on me. I hate to sound like a male chauvinist pig, but here was a woman who, if you unscrewed her back, would reveal a mainspring, some nuts and bolts, and one or two moving parts, but little else. And I could have wished for something more because it was for want of a strong mother that Richie's father had come to dominate him so completely. Oh, Sondra tried to provide the missing feminine influence but when a sister tries to be a mother she ends up acting more like a wife.

Sondra and Richie both hung back as if they wanted to talk to me privately. I wanted to speak to Richie but I felt it best not to indulge in sentimentality with Sondra. She looked at me with round, hazy, sad eyes and pouting mouth. I took her hand, squeezed it tenderly, and kissed her on the cheek. Then I gently nudged her toward the metal-detection chamber through which all boarding passengers must pass and from which there was no return. "I hope you're not packing a gun," I said. "They'll have you arrested as a potential skyjacker."

"If I was packing one, I know who I'd use it on. Dave, listen—"

"No, *you* listen. I'm an old-fashioned Southern gentleman and I was brought up with some pretty antebellum notions about women, such as they fall into two categories: nice girls—the kind you marry—and the other kind."

"That's not antebellum, that's antediluvian," she sighed.

"Be that as it may, you unfortunately fall into the nice-girl category. I say 'unfortunately' because I'm not ready to settle down again and I don't feel like using you the other way. Also, you have some growing up to do. So why don't we leave it at that. I'm sure I'll be seeing you again because of your brother. We'll look at ourselves then and see. How does that sound?"

"Shitty," she said, her voice echoing the word in the metal-detection chamber like some awful pronouncement from on high. And it was to echo in my head for weeks.

I turned away.

Richie was standing against the wall and I sidled over to him. He looked at the bandage on my cheek and shook his head. "I heard about Timmie Lee," he said.

"From whom?"

"From your friend Roy Lescade. He came over to the hotel before we left for the airport. Mr. Bolt, I'd like to send a check to Timmie's family, maybe start a scholarship fund or something. What do you think?"

"I think that would be fitting and proper." I took a cigar out of my pocket and lit it. "What did you tell Roy?"

"What you told me to tell him. That I'd had a fight with Vreel over the question of a big loan and that I'd been in seclusion while you were hammering out a compromise."

"What did Roy say about that?"

"He said it was just another ho-hum story about a contract squabble. He's not even going to bother writing it up."

"He bought it, huh?"

"Sure," Richie smiled. "I'm very convincing, you know."

"So I've observed. You have honesty credits with Roy, I guess."

He laughed, but wistfully. "Do I have any with you?"

"Uh uh. They're all spent. You'll have to start banking them again."

I fixed my eyes on his, hoping even at this last moment to secure some kind of concrete confirmation that it was he and no one else who had collaborated with Stanley Vreel. But all I saw was my reflection in the glacial blue of his irises.

"What's going to happen, Mr. Bolt?"

I shrugged. "What's going to happen is that Stanley Vreel will soon announce that his franchise is up for sale. By autumn you'll be playing under new management, maybe in another city. And maybe for less money."

I watched his reactions. There were none. He simply said, "I see."

Yet he lingered even as his parents and Sondra shouted

to him to hurry. "Is there something you wanted to talk to me about?" I said.

He fidgeted for a minute, his eyes roving around the terminal, his mouth slightly puckered in thought. Finally, he said, "This is going to sound a little flaky, Mr. Bolt, but—have you ever been in analysis?"

"No, why?"

"I was just wondering what it's like, that's all."

"You think you might need it?" My pulse had quickened and I felt a strange, quiet happiness inside.

"Me? Of course not. Haven't you heard? I'm perfect!" There was a glimmer of mockery in his eyes, self-mockery, perhaps the first such glimmer he'd ever had.

"I think it might be very helpful to you," I said. "Maybe your recent 'ordeal' has made you think about yourself. Analysis might help you see things more clearly."

"Things that *you* see about me, you mean?"

"Yes, things that I see about you."

He picked up his overnight bag. "You're really a good guy, Mr. Bolt."

"I'm just your agent," I said, shaking his hand.

A Look At: Death In the Crease (The Pro Book Two)

In the cutthroat, glamorous world of professional sports, one man works behind the scenes to fix his superstar clients' biggest problems: agent Dave Bolt.

Officially, Dave Bolt is a sports agent, representing professional athletes in basketball, football, baseball, hockey—you name it. Unofficially, he is a kind of undercover operator, a troubleshooter for a number of pro sports organizations.

Bolt's walk on the dark side starts with one phone call concerning the hottest basketball prospect in the country. It ends with a hairline fracture of his cheekbone, temporary blindness, a scrotum full of someone's knee, and the loss of the most promising marital prospect since his divorce. Oh, and a commission of staggering proportions.

AVAILABLE OCTOBER 2020

About the Author

Though Richard Curtis is best known as a leading New York literary agent, he is also author of dozens of works of fiction and nonfiction published by leading publishers, as well as numerous works of humor and award-winning satire. His plays have been performed in numerous venues and festivals in New York. He is currently writing, producing and directing The Creepery, a series of horror podcasts scheduled for launch late in 2020.

Curtis's interest in emerging media and technology led to his founding of the first commercial e-book publishing company in the English language seven years before the introduction of the Kindle and the Digital Revolution.

Curtis was the first president of the Independent Literary Agents Association and was President of the Association of Authors' Representatives in 1996 and 1997.

Early in his freelance career he conceived The Pro, featuring a sports agent sleuth and action hero (modeled after Dallas Cowboys quarterback Don Meredith). Unlike his book's hero, Curtis is not very good with his fists.

Made in the USA
Middletown, DE
21 September 2020